Advance Praise for

"Alan Heathcock's voice is the American voice, doing what it was meant to do. It's full of distance and wind, highways and heart. He's the real deal."

—Luis Alberto Urrea, author of *Into the Beautiful North*

"The stories in *Volt* are rich in surprise moments of brightness and bleakness, told in strong straight sentences. Alan Heathcock has a cowpoke's eye for the bloom and detritus of the landscape, and language that puts one right there in the picture, banging through the greasewood, the cornfield, crossing the flats and sudden gullies. These are tough and potent stories, deeply felt and imagined. Heathcock is a writer who goes without flinching into the darker corners of human experience, but has the grace to bring any available light with him."

—Daniel Woodrell, author of *Winter's Bone* and *Tomato Red*

"Alan Heathcock is an epic storyteller—and *Volt* is an epic collection. You will come away from each of these majestic stories thrilled, alternately terrified and heartened, ultimately full of wonder at how the author manages to make twenty pages so timeless, so deep and sweeping—every story like a novel writ small."

—Benjamin Percy, author of *The Wilding* and *Refresh, Refresh*

"In the tradition of Breece D'J Pancake and Kent Meyers, Alan Heathcock turns his small town into a big canvas. Like the tales in *Winesburg, Ohio*, the stories in *Volt* are full of violence and regret, and the sad desperation of the grotesque."

—Stewart O'Nan, author of *Songs for the Missing*

VOLT

VOLT

Stories

Alan Heathcock

Graywolf Press

"The Staying Freight" first appeared in the *Harvard Review*.
"Smoke" first appeared in the *Kenyon Review*.
"Furlough" first appeared in *Storyville*.
"Peacekeeper" first appeared in the *Virginia Quarterly Review*.
"Fort Apache" first appeared in *Zoetrope: All-Story*.

This publication is made possible by funding provided in part by a grant from the Minnesota State Arts Board, through an appropriation by the Minnesota State Legislature, a grant from the National Endowment for the Arts, and private funders. Significant support has also been provided by Target; the McKnight Foundation; and other generous contributions from foundations, corporations, and individuals. To these organizations and individuals we offer our heartfelt thanks.

NATIONAL ENDOWMENT FOR THE ARTS   MINNESOTA STATE ARTS BOARD   WELLS FARGO   TARGET.

Published by Graywolf Press
250 Third Avenue North, Suite 600
Minneapolis, Minnesota 55401

All rights reserved.

www.graywolfpress.org

Published in the United States of America

ISBN 978-1-55597-577-7

2 4 6 8 9 7 5 3 1
First Graywolf Printing, 2011

Library of Congress Control Number: 2010937515

Cover design: Kyle G. Hunter

Cover photo: Vstock LLC / Getty Images

For Rochelle

CONTENTS

The Staying Freight   3

Smoke   41

Peacekeeper   61

Furlough   85

Fort Apache   97

The Daughter   115

Lazarus   163

Volt   181

VOLT

THE STAYING FREIGHT

I

Dusk burned the ridgeline and dust churned from the tiller discs set a fog over the field. He blinked, could not stop blinking. There was not a clean part on him with which to wipe his eyes. Tomorrow he'd reserved for the sowing of winter wheat and so much was yet to be done. Thirty-eight and well respected, always brought dry grain to store, as sure a thing as a farmer could be. This was Winslow Nettles.

Winslow simply didn't see his boy running across the field. He didn't see Rodney climb onto the back of the tractor, hands filled with meatloaf and sweet corn wrapped in foil. Didn't see Rodney's boot slide off the hitch.

Winslow dabbed his eyes with a filthy handkerchief. The tiller discs hopped. He whirled to see what he'd plowed, and back there lay a boy like something fallen from the sky.

Winslow leapt from the tractor, ran to his son. With his belt, he cinched a gash in the boy's leg. He pressed his palm to Rodney's neck. Blood purled between his fingers. Winslow cradled his son in his lap and watched the tractor roll on, tilling a fading arc of dust toward the freight rail tracks that marked the northern end of all that was his.

2

Lights flashed and bells dinged. Winslow stopped his truck at the crossing. A freight engine emerged from the woods, shuddered around the bend. Winslow eyed the train's iron wheels, eyed the hillside beyond the tracks, his old clapboard house, round-roofed barn, grain silos perched above the barley. The train chugged nearer. It'd take twenty minutes to pass. Winslow had thirty-seven acres to swath, had lost so much time with his boy's death, with the funeral and relatives, with long hours holding his wife, Sadie, so many tears she'd cried, so much water in one woman.

The crossing shook. The freight horn shrieked, wailing louder, nearer. Winslow stomped the accelerator. The truck lurched onto the tracks and the engine's nose filled his window. He jerked the wheel and the pickup swerved, rocked, but stayed on the road. He sped up the hill, boxcars flashing in his rearview mirror, train brakes screeching and freight joints howling as the line clawed to a halt.

From high in his combine, Winslow eyed the dormant train, the engine far to the west, the coal cars deep into the eastern woods. An hour had passed and there it sat. Winslow's nerves were frayed. He turned his gaze to the reels cutting under the barley. Blackbirds burst from the field. From the corner of his eye, Winslow noticed a flash of white in the crop, then a crouching man sprang and dashed in front of the harrower.

Winslow yanked the brake, struck his head against the back window. His pulse thumped in his throat as he shut down the combine.

Then someone was pounding on the cab, and there stood a man, out of breath, in a white dress shirt under soiled gray coveralls. Winslow threw open the door, hopped down into the field.

"What the hell you doing, mister?" Winslow shouted.

The man pressed nose to nose with Winslow. His eyes were flushed as if from weeping, his hair white as the moon, and a scar split his lips and curled like a pig's tail onto his cheek.

"Could've killed you," he lisped.

Winslow glanced at the combine. "I could've killed *you*."

"You son of a bitch," the man barked. "I'm giving you a taste of your own."

"Watch your mouth, mister," Winslow said. "You don't know me from Adam."

The man took Winslow by his overall straps and slung him to the ground. He stood over Winslow, noon sun glinting off sweat in the curl of his scar. "Ain't gonna do it no more," the train man said, pointing down in Winslow's face. "So you just go to hell."

The wind blew the man's hair up into white flames. Winslow set his jaw, thought the man would strike him. Instead, the freight man stood tall, raised the zipper of his coveralls, and took off running.

Winslow watched him sprint up the slope, away from the tracks, away from his train. He ran high-kneed through the barley, past Winslow's house, past the barn and silos, never stopping, never looking back. Soon he was a speck on the horizon, and, as if slipping through a pinhole in the sky, the freight man was over the ridge and gone.

3

For a long time, Winslow sat in the barley, determined to finish his work. But then, his hands shaking, eyes pulsing, he was overcome by a fever. It'd taken all his will just to return to the house.

Now Winslow gathered himself in the foyer. He slumped against a wall, listening to the squeak of a chair. In the front parlor, a wood-paneled room that was dark despite bay windows, Sadie worked needlepoint, yarn draping the sofa, purples and reds and golds unfurled about her rocking chair.

"Taking a break," Winslow called, and hurried back to the kitchen. His eyes burned. His temples throbbed. He pulled open the freezer door and out tumbled frozen peas. Winslow slid down the fridge to the tile floor. He held the peas to his face.

"Hungry, Win?" Sadie asked from the hall, her footsteps approaching, and then she was in the kitchen. *"Win?"*

Winslow closed his eyes, could feel her at his side, her hot hand on his neck, the other on his forehead.

"Oh, Win," she said. "You're burning up."

Sadie was a furnace blasted over him. Her fingers seared his cheeks, his throat. He pleaded, *"Leave me be,"* then *"Please, hon,"* but she wouldn't move, and the heat rose up in him, his shoulders quaking, his arms.

Winslow thrust his hands against Sadie. She tripped, fell hard against the kitchen table, tumbled to the floor. She lay under the table, clutching her skull.

Winslow rushed to her. "Hon," he said, afraid to touch her. "I'm so sorry, hon."

Sadie turned a cheek against the tile, pulled her hand from her hair. Blood streaked her palm.

Winslow lay awake, aware of his muscles, of his heavy breathing, the groan of the bedsprings. The doctor had given Sadie painkillers and she slept soundly beside him. A swath of her hair had been shaved, her stitches stained orange from the iodine.

Now and forever I'll be the man what killed his boy. A man what shoved his wife. Winslow wanted to wake Sadie and apologize again and again. He was so riled. He rolled gently out of bed and fumbled in the darkness with his overalls and boots.

Winslow bumped down the hall to a door they now kept locked. As a drunk warns himself from a tavern, he'd warned himself from this room. He set his forehead against the door, trying to remember Rodney's face. But only the freight man came to mind, that white hair, the man running, receding through the barley.

Sweat beaded upon Winslow's brow. He hurried into the bathroom and splashed cold water over his face. Again he recalled the freight man shrinking on the ridge, vanishing.

Winslow stepped to the doorway. Moonlight from the parlor trailed up the stairs. He crossed the hall, peered down into the glow. Sadie had removed all the photos of Rodney from the stairwell, and as Winslow descended he traced his fingertips over the nails on which they'd hung.

The front parlor was washed in moonlight. Winslow stepped to the bay window. The land outside was bright. He let his eyes drift far down the slope of barley. At the field's base crouched the wall of train, a lampblack silhouette, a driverless freight.

Why hadn't they come for it? Wouldn't someone miss it by now? Blood ticked in Winslow's skull. The train man's scarred cheek bristled in his mind. That man just ran away. He just left.

Winslow hurried to the kitchen and rummaged through drawers for a notepad and pen. He didn't know what to write. He scribbled: *Took a walk. Be back soon.*

Winslow read it once, considered its meaning. He had no plan. Just to walk. To settle himself a bit. Winslow folded the paper. He held it to his lips then left it on the kitchen table.

4

Winslow kicked through the barley. Hill after hill he hiked, eyes always on the next knob. At the edge of his field, he allowed himself to glance back over his shoulder. He'd trod a path of shadow through the crop. Only the silver dome of his silo was visible above the ridge.

He hopped a ditch and pushed between rows of chest-high corn. Atop a bald knob, Winslow found the brightest light on the horizon, what he thought was from a radio tower, but was actually Venus low in the night, and decided he'd only rest when it burned directly overhead.

He crossed a reeking field of mint, a cow pasture, slogged through a muddy pea field. Hours of steady travel found him passing homes of people he'd never met.

On and on he went until, walking through the ropy branches in a grove of willow trees, speckles of dawn's half-light warmed his face. Winslow rubbed his thighs, considered turning back. But I'll snap, he thought. Hurt Sadie again. I'll just take a day to get my head right. Sadie'll understand. It's for her. For us.

Winslow needed wilderness, needed solitude. But wherever he turned there was a dirt road, the whir of a sewage treatment plant, a bait store's roof winking in the sun. By noon he stood on a bluff above the wide river that marked the state line. He sidetracked an hour before a rusty trestle gave passage to the other side. Winslow peered between rotting ties as he crossed over the churning brown water, clutching girders until safely aground again.

His ankles were swollen, the balls of his feet blistered. He rested beneath the bridge, stuffed grass into his boot heels and tightened his laces. He hobbled along the berm until pawpaw smothered the shore and the hills seemed untouched. Winslow bulled through overgrowth, limbs scraping his cheeks, burrs biting his socks, his neck and forearms barked by brambles.

Deep in the interior, he rested atop a hardwood knob overlooking a thread of brook. Sunlight bucked on the water. Though his body was still, his mind reeled in flashes: a child's boot upright in a rut; a nurse cutting away Sadie's bloody hair; a man's crooked finger in his face.

Dusk descended and the moon crawled into the trees. Winslow crouched in nightshade, his pocketknife drawn. He figured Sadie had called the neighbors looking for him, possibly called the police, and imagined her working needlepoint and listening for footsteps on the porch. He wept and listened to the woods come to life and didn't sleep.

Dawn bloomed gray green, thunderheads shrouding the hills. It was time to go home, but Winslow's feet were very sore, the walk back so far.

What'll I tell Sadie? he wondered. That I didn't trust you to understand my tears? That I thought you'd see me as weak for the rest of our goddamn lives if I wept just a little? His tiredness was a ballast around his neck, and Winslow tucked his arms into his bibs, eyes closed, and stood that way atop the wooded hill.

Drizzle tapped his eyelids. The rain quickened to a downpour and Winslow scrambled beneath a sandstone ledge. Rain stung sideways, the hill's grass blown flat. The brook slowly swelled, roiling into whitecaps. Mud crept up the slope. When the sun finally burned through the clouds, Winslow was famished. He searched the woods and found bushes overspread with opal berries. He greedily ate them, couldn't swallow them fast enough.

Soon his stomach seized. He vomited. Once again, he shivered with fever. His skin steamed. Winslow stripped naked and, holding an exposed tree root, allowed his body to drag in the cold brook. The gap was lost in shadow, and clutching the root, brown water rushing about his chin, he saw a figure atop the hill, the train man backlit by dusk.

The man stood away from the tree, held up a hand, and waved

down. Winslow felt as if something giving chase had finally caught him. He shut his eyes and waited for a hand to pull him from the water and drag him back home. Winslow refused to open his eyes. On and on he waited, but the expected pull never came.

Winslow woke covered in mud. It was a new morning, the sun scorching, the brook receding into its banks. Winslow climbed the hill, found no footprints, no evidence at all of the train man's visit. But the feeling of being pursued remained. He quickly dressed and fled south. At the base of each ridge he thought of Sadie and felt he should backtrack, should begin the long walk home. But then his weary knees lifted, and he stepped up one rock, and then the next.

Deep in the night, after walking all day and on through the evening without a bite to eat, he came upon a yellow tent beside a white truck. Winslow shooed raccoons from a picnic table, devoured stale hot dog buns. Someone moved in the tent, and Winslow stuffed his pockets with pretzel twists, ran clutching a red box of graham crackers.

He raced without direction through the woods, then the trees opened and he crossed a highway, headlights covering him, brake lights flashing, and the land changed again as he dashed headlong into a dark treeless canyon.

Weeks he wandered, awake day and night, eating berries and cress, beetles and worms, an occasional fish, a groundhog caught with his bare hands. Though Winslow's mind hadn't reconciled, his body had evolved. At first he'd always been tired, but now he walked vigorously, all day and without pain. His limbs grew sleek, stomach ribbed with granite, beard and hair tangled and sunbleached, skin baked into a russet hide.

The first leaves began to turn and Winslow wondered if maybe his grief would fade with the season. Sunburn no longer affected him, and as the autumn air cooled he did not shiver, and therefore believed he'd tapped some vein man had long since lost beneath quilts and down comforters.

Not a day went by he didn't consider going home. Some days he'd backtrack a mile, sometimes longer, before a quake of anguish turned him away again.

One tin-skied day, the rain upon hollyhock conjured the scent of Sadie's perfume. Winslow ran weeping in the direction he believed led home, ran all afternoon and into the night, stopping only when confronted by a wall of peaks. There was no way around; the first time through had taken two full days to scale and descend.

Winslow dropped to his knees. In his periphery he glimpsed a presence, and believed the train man had again found him. But when he turned he saw only a scraggly pine rising from the rock.

Winslow hurled stones at the little tree. Wrung its trunk as if it were a throat. He flailed and throttled the sapling to the ground. Winslow hugged its limbs and tried to weep, but was, at last, dry of tears. Under a pale moon, Winslow knew he no longer belonged to the world of men and would forever roam the woods as a lost son of the civil.

5

Winslow trailed loons to a stumpy lake and sat on a log, watching the shallows and plotting to catch his supper. The setting sun nestled in the treetops. Beyond the loons, packs of pintails and canvasbacks bobbed on red-tinged water.

A flurry of ducks took wing. They flew toward the sun and banked high above. A shotgun fired upshore. A duck dropped from the chevron, tumbling down and down to thud in the cattails at Winslow's feet. Its head shimmered like green metal, one wing broken beneath its body. He lifted the bird, its neck flopped over his fingers, body still warm, tail feathers damp.

Quickly came a breaking in the reeds and a hound had Winslow's arm in its teeth. The dog thrashed its head. Winslow dropped the duck, yanked the dog up into a bear hug. The hound snapped at Winslow's face and Winslow squeezed and the dog yelped.

Orange flashed from the reeds. A hunter swung his rifle, its stock exploding against Winslow's jaw. Then Winslow was on his back, his vision blurred. He rose to flee. He staggered, his legs failing as cattails rushed at his face.

Winslow woke to sparks in his vision. Searing pain spiked his eyes. He lay in the hull of a metal boat, his hands and feet bound with fishing line, his jaw so swollen he couldn't lift his head.

Clouds slid passing, the sky graying to night. Soon came cypress branches draped with moss, a dock's haloed light. The hull scraped the shore. The hunter dragged the boat onto land, each tug a sledge to the spike in Winslow's skull.

Solitary minutes passed, but the pain in his face kept Winslow from trying to move. Then three men stood over him. One at each elbow, the other at his boots, they lifted him from the boat and carried him to a truck bed stinking of fish.

They drove slowly, but the road was rutted and Winslow moaned against the jostling. They hauled him into a tiny stone building, onto a cot in a cell with metal bars.

They cut his bindings. Winslow didn't struggle. The men retreated to folding chairs outside the bars. The man in hunter's orange was rotund and horse-faced, his cheeks ruddy and whiskerless. Beside him, a man sat cross-legged, dark gouges for eyes, dressed head to toe in lawman's tan. The third, his old flesh the same color as his smoke-stained dentures, said slowly and loudly, "This—is—Barclay—County."

Winslow tried to speak, to say who he was, but his jaw was destroyed, his words gibberish.

"See them eyes?" the old man said to the others. "That boy's wild as the wind."

A gaunt man with pomaded hair carried in a black satchel and stood beside Winslow's cot. The lawman was there, too. He used his pistol to part the beard on Winslow's chin. The doctor squinted over Winslow. "It's busted terrible," he said to the lawman. "Hand me my bag."

Winslow searched the man's eyes for intent.

"Easy now, fella," the doctor said down to him, like calming a mule. Winslow felt alcohol cool his biceps. A needle jabbed him.

He stared up at the cracked ceiling. A moth flitted about a light shielded in wire. Soon the light blurred, the moth became lambent confetti, and his heavy lids closed.

6

Daylight shone through a barred window high up the wall. Winslow batted his eyes, tried to focus himself. Tiny wires secured shut his mouth. He gingerly ran his fingers over the wires, over his teeth. He knew it was over. He wondered what would happen to him now.

The doctor entered the cell. In his shirt pocket was a prescription pad. Winslow lifted his hand, pointed at the pad, wiggled his hand denoting his desire to write. The doctor glanced to the door, where the lawman stood. The lawman tapped a thumb against his teeth. He nodded to the doctor. Winslow took the pad and pen from the doctor.

He wrote: *I MEAN NO HARM.*

The truth would send him home. He couldn't go home. So Winslow wrote that his name was Red, that he'd been a rancher before some big company bought his cattle and cut him loose. At some point he'd decided to hike the woods. *BEEN LOST A LONG TIME.* As the doctor read aloud, Winslow had the sensation Sadie stood just beyond the cell bars, hearing all these lies. He couldn't fight it off and began to cry.

The lawman patted Winslow's boot. "Any family we can call?"

Winslow pressed the pen point to his lips. He thought long on how to respond. Finally, he scrawled: *ALL DEAD.*

He heard only murmurs of their discussion out in the hall. Then the lawman, whose name was Bently, came in and motioned at the hunter trailing him, explained that since Ham had busted Winslow's jaw he'd volunteered to take him in. Winslow could stay in a trailer at Ham's farm. If he felt up to it, he could work the turkeys, make a few bucks.

"Just until you get back on your feet," Bently said. "But you're a free man. Can leave now if you'd like."

Winslow stared out the cell window. The sky was a dark, wet snow dripping down the glass. He knew it'd be tough in the woods with his jaw broke. Ham, eyes full of regret, smiled at him.

Winslow scratched the pad as if etching the word in stone: *WORK.*

7

They drove crumbling roads up into the hills. Winslow wore a new jacket, overalls, socks, and boots, a sack filled with canned soup in his lap, all bought by Ham, an advance from his first paycheck.

"Turkey's the future," Ham said, having talked without pause the entire way from town. "Folks want *healthy*. They want turkey. Nutritious as an apple. More versatile than chicken. It's the future, buddy, and that ain't just talk. Got fifty ways to put turkey in the place of beef and pork—" and he began going one by one down the list.

Soon they turned onto a dirt lane between leafless stands of ash and bounced into a clearing that was the farm. A corral of turkeys sprang to life, black feathers shifting, the birds shrieking. Beyond the corral sagged a weathered barn. They drove behind it and parked beside a silver trailer wedged between spruce trees, the trailer vertically dented from the trees, which bowed over the fuselage like weary giants.

"Keep her here to block the wind," Ham said, like an apology. "Don't look like much, but she'll keep the cold off you."

The warmth of blankets made Winslow uneasy. Back in the woods, he'd constantly been gripped by figuring how to keep a fire, how to fend off mosquitoes, how to find water and know it was clean. Now Winslow's mind teemed with thoughts of home.

This time of year, Ced Raney always had an Oktoberfest party in his barn, and Winslow worried how people spoke of him in his absence. He thought of Jon Debuque, a bachelor who'd had eyes for Sadie ever since high school, and imagined Sadie crying in her rocker and Jon stroking her hair, telling her he'd make everything all right.

Winslow threw off the covers and rushed out of the trailer. Icy wind braised his skin. The frozen dirt burned his toes. Winslow stepped to the spruce. He held a branch and crawled beneath the limbs. Lying on his back, trembling on the bed of needles, Winslow peered up into the tree's cold wavering guts.

At daybreak, truck lights bobbled into the clearing. Winslow was relieved the night was done. He hustled into the trailer and dressed, and met Ham as he climbed from his truck, as did a boy, a teenaged version of Ham, and an ample woman in a denim jumper. Ham introduced them as Jim and Sheila, his son and his wife. Winslow shook Sheila's hand, and Jim stared dumbly at Winslow's wired jaw.

Winslow followed Ham into the corral. Turkeys woke gobbling as Ham kicked them out of the way. They entered the old barn. A large section of roof was missing. Through the gap the snow came gently down. Ham turned his face to the sky, tried to catch snowflakes on his tongue. Then he smacked his lips, looked over at Winslow.

"Red?" he said. "How you feel about killing?"

8

The turkeys were so loud Winslow hadn't heard the boys enter the barn. He carried a bird under his arm and watched Ham's son, Jim, lead several boys up a ladder. One by one, they disappeared into the loft.

All morning he'd worked without a break. Pegs all along the back wall were hung with bleeding carcasses. Then Winslow stepped to the block and threw down the bird. He lifted a cleaver, chopped its neck. Its head fell into a bucket and its body flailed, flailed, fluttered to still.

Something wet struck Winslow's cheek. He heard laughter from above. He looked up, found the boys silhouetted against the hole in the roof. One in a yellow cap waved to Winslow. The boy hawked, spat again. All the boys laughed. Winslow kept his eyes on that yellow cap. He raised the cleaver high. Off came the turkey's feet.

At lunchtime, Winslow walked out into the corral. The boys were waiting for him. He passed cautiously through the pack. The one in the yellow cap stepped forward. He was lanky but well muscled, acne pocking his cheeks. "Pleased to meet you, new guy," he said. He gave a snaggled grin, extended his hand.

Winslow moved to shake his hand. The boy lunged to punch Winslow's gut. Winslow tensed and the fist struck awkward. The boy fell clutching his arm. Winslow knelt over the boy, who wailed, rolling about, the bone of his broken wrist pressing the skin.

Ham raced through the birds and screamed, "What the hell's going on?"

Jim pointed at the boy on the ground. "Was Harold's idea," he told his father. "Harold wanted to see how the new man would holler with his mouth wired shut."

That night, Winslow followed Ham into Barney's Tap, a shotgun bar with its doors left open though it was cold. Ham felt bad about what happened with the boys and set up a game of poker as a show of goodwill. A dozen or so people drank in the bar. They all eyed Winslow as he sat across from the lawman, Bently, and Rico, the old man from the jail.

They played with peanuts worth a dime. Winslow motioned for cards, knocked the table to bump, found he didn't need to talk. He lifted a bottle to his mouth and beer trickled between his teeth. After several bottles, Winslow was drunk in a room full of strangers. He passed a note to Rico, who smiled his denture smile and held the note at arm's length to read. "Red says he had him a son."

"A son?" Ham said. "Where's he gone off to?"

"Don't be ignorant, Ham." Bently looked Winslow in the eye, as to say he didn't need to respond.

Winslow scribbled *WHISKEY,* handed the paper to Ham.

A voice hollered his name. No, not his name. The voice hollered *Red.* Winslow turned to the voice. His eyesight bleared, he could barely make out Ham in the bar's back door. Winslow stumbled to stand and banged his way through tables to lean on the wall beside Ham.

"Need you to meet some fellas," Ham slurred, staggering down three steps into a dark grassless lot.

Two young men waited outside. One wore a thin beard and smoked against the stoop rail. The other had an upturned nose, like a snout, and eyes that didn't blink. Winslow stepped down by Ham. The pig man balled a fist. Winslow instinctively tightened. The punch cracked like a dry branch, and the man ran in circles with his wrist between his thighs, dropped to the dirt like an animal shot.

Ham hugged Winslow's neck. "Told you my boy's a rock," he cackled into the night. "A goddamn human rock."

The next day, Ham sauntered across the barn, hands stuffed in the pockets of his coveralls. Winslow saw him coming and turned to the wall of pegs, his mind fuzzed from smoke and whiskey, and peered into a turkey's dull feathers.

"Jesus, Red," Ham said. "How many times I got to apologize?"

Winslow stepped to the chopping block.

"I got a deal for you," Ham said. "So just hear me out."

Winslow gripped the cleaver, gave Ham his eyes.

"You're about the toughest fella I ever knew. And now"—he jutted a thumb out at the corral—"these kids want to bet a hundred bucks their boy can knock the wind from you with a punch." Ham rapped his knuckles on the block. "I know this boy. He's big as a bus, and just as big a pansy," he said. "What say, Red? Forty for me, sixty for you?"

Winslow's hands glistened with blood. He disgusted himself. I deserve this much, he thought. He lay down the cleaver, nodded to Ham.

Winslow followed Ham out to the gate where the boys bounded about like puppies. One boy, a head taller than the others and wide as a door, threw off a green and gold letterman's jacket and flexed a meaty fist. Ham stood Winslow against the fence. The boy hulked before him.

"This is for Harold," he hissed.

Winslow nodded he was ready.

A roundhouse like a brick on a chain flung Winslow against the fence and he tripped forward but kept his feet. He exhaled through his teeth. Inhaled with ease. Ham's voice rang over the lot of cussing boys, *"That's my wild man. That's my rock."*

9

Ham announced in Barney's he'd give the highest bidder a chance to punch Winslow in the stomach, promising to double the money if the person could knock his wild man clean out of wind. Winslow listened from the back door, Bently smoking a pipe out on the stoop.

"You all right with this, Red?" the lawman asked.

Winslow shrugged.

"Ham gets bad ideas breakfast, lunch, and dinner. I'll make him stop if you like."

Winslow wrote on his pad: *DON'T CARE.*

Just after midnight, Winslow braced himself against the long oak bar, and a red-nosed man in a VFW ball cap flailed at his gut. Winslow didn't budge, didn't blink. The small crowd chortled and shrieked and Ham cried in Winslow's ear, *"Sixty bucks, lickety-split."*

Nightly biddings drew new faces: a foundry worker missing an ear; a bent old woman mumbling her dead husband's name; a man in a white-collared shirt, his fist wrapped in a gabardine scarf; an elementary school teacher apologizing before she swung, wild-eyed and cursing Winslow after.

The crowds grew, and Ham cornered off a stage with chicken wire mounted with trouble lights. Winslow stood bare-chested in the harsh light. Ham, in an ill-fitting suit, a felt hat adorned with turkey feathers, rang a bell and shouted, "Our world's turned polite, some might say *dainty*. We all know how things used to be, men uprooting trees with their hands and backs, women fighting off panthers with hairpins and a mother's scorn. Those days are gone, my friends," and he paused, eyeing them all. "Yet you still got that rage inside you, don't you? *Don't you?* Well, that's why you're here. Who'll start us at a hundred even?"

Winslow watched faces barking bids. The man who won stepped around the chicken wire, wore horn-rimmed glasses, tugged long hair behind his pierced ears. In this young man's lenses Winslow saw his own reflection: a lockjawed, feral-haired savage. He prepared his body. The punch was thrown. Winslow took a breath. He always took a breath.

10

In Barney's bathroom, Ham smeared charcoal beneath Winslow's eyes, told him to growl through his wires, stamp a foot onstage. Winslow followed Ham into the bar, through men in stocking caps, beers in gloved fists, not even the blizzard outside thinning the crowd.

The same storm had earlier in the day bayed over Winslow's trailer, the sky whirling like a snow globe shaken. He'd sat in the trailer's window, imagining the shuddering room was a train engine, a crossing and a truck on the tracks ahead. He saw his own face in the truck window, anticipating the crushing of metal and glass and bone.

Winslow carried that same doom as he stepped onto the stage, his mind plagued by questions. Would it matter if it weren't my fault? Could I let it go if I knew what's to blame? How do I aim these ugly thoughts to be rid of them?

He stood before the chicken wire, before faces breathing steam in the cold barroom. Ham drew a riding crop from inside his jacket and lashed Winslow across his naked back. Winslow arched his spine, glared hard at Ham as the audience howled.

"Don't turn them crazy eyes on me," Ham scolded out the side of his mouth. "Ain't me what's going to pay."

Winslow lay in the examination room. Through grimed windows, he watched the flurried sky, a string of colored lights swinging from the clinic's eaves. A knock came on the door. Six weeks he'd worn the wires and now they were gone.

Winslow flexed his jaw, formed the words, "Come in."

Ham entered, hat in hand, and stood beside a little Christmas tree in the corner of the room. "Strange to talk?"

Winslow nodded. "Jaw's rusty."

"You feeling strong?"

"I feel all right."

"Good. I'm glad." Ham stared into the tree, hung his cap on a branch. "Got the Christmas birds sold," he said, and stepped to the window. He tapped the sill, smiled down at Winslow. "You look good, Red. Look strong."

Winslow knew what was on Ham's mind. "I want a steak," he said. "Get me a steak. But go ahead and tell folks I'll be on tonight."

"All right." Ham patted Winslow's leg. "Rico and me," he said, and stared at the door. "We thought it best you don't talk during the show. It's just folks don't see you as a real man."

Wind whistled off the eaves. "I won't say nothing," Winslow said, the colored lights madly twirling. "Just get me a steak. I'll eat it with my hands if you want. Eat it right there on stage."

Her blouse read *Delsea's Cafe,* and below that *Lilian.* Ham asked Winslow if he was ready. Winslow just stared at the woman, dismayed by the resemblance; the same build as Sadie, face with the same tapered chin, same sad brown eyes, and she wore a silver chain and cross just like Sadie.

Her fist popped weakly off Winslow. Those in the bar laughed and hooted. Lilian looked at her fist. Slowly her body shook, as she started to sob.

Even her tears fell like Sadie's.

"I'll get your money back," Winslow blurted. "Buy yourself something nice. Some jewelry or a sweater or something. Something nice. Something—" He pulled her to him, her cheek pressed tightly to his pounding heart.

Lilian shrieked. She struggled to get loose and Winslow held her tighter. A wicked smack stung Winslow across his bare shoulders. Ham yanked Lilian free, waving the riding crop at Winslow as a tamer might ward off a lion.

II

Winslow paced the dark trailer. He realized, with the reclamation of his voice, he could simply phone Sadie. But it was very late. He had no phone. I'll go to town in the morning, he told himself. Can hear Sadie's voice this very day. I can tell her where I'm at, that I don't know how I got here. It wouldn't be a complete lie. He could tell her he wanted to come home. Could say he was lost without her. He'd say as many true things as he could before she hung up.

"Something nice," he said, aloud. "Something *nice*," searching for perfect kindness in his tone.

Then Winslow remembered Lilian's revolted expression and knew his voice couldn't mute his appearance. I'll get a haircut. A shave. I'll become myself again.

But then old fears took hold. Sadie won't want to hear from me. She's glad I'm gone. She's glad I ain't around to remind her of her dead boy. Winslow dropped to the floor. He grunted out sit-ups, counting aloud to dissuade thought, shouting numbers in the cold, dank trailer.

Bitter wind whipped Winslow's hair in his eyes. He cowered behind the red-striped pole in the building's alcove. Then the old barber was there, waving Winslow aside to unlock the door. Winslow trailed the man into the dark shop.

"Ain't got a dime to spare to you," the barber said to him.

"I got money."

The old man nodded, suspicious. Then he threw the lights and put on his white smock. He walked behind a chair and brushed the seat with a whisk. Winslow sat down. The barber secured the cape and stood before Winslow, his eyes wide like a man figuring how to clear a prairie.

"What'll it be?"

Winslow stared at a Christmas wreath hung in the front window. "Used to be a farmer," he said. "Was a deacon at my church."

"All right then," the barber said. "Deacon it is."

The barber clipped the beard at Winslow's throat. Outside, the sun glared off the snowy road. Three boys passed, each holding a cigarette to his lips. One boy, heavily jowled for his age, glanced in the window. Winslow heard the lather dispenser, felt the cream hot down his neck. The boys stood in the window, smoking, watching.

"Ain't there school around here?" Winslow asked.

The barber turned, straight razor poised. "Not all's meant for learning," he said, and leaned over Winslow, squinting as the blade shaved the cream. Winslow felt the air chill his skin, felt the boys' eyes on his bare throat.

Bing Crosby singing "Silver Bells" played on the radio in Delsea's Café. Winslow watched Lilian refill a man's cup at the end of the counter. She'd refilled his own cup three times, had looked him square in the face, but with his haircut and shave she'd not recognized him. Winslow held a five-dollar bill, stared long at its edges, then raised it high. Lilian walked down, coffeepot in hand. Winslow handed her the money.

"Change this for quarters?" he asked.

"Want any bills back?"

He shook his head. "Got a call to make. Need the coins."

Lilian made change at the register, then Winslow pushed out the café door, the quarters jingling in his pocket. He passed an alley, where the boys from the barbershop huddled smoking. He crossed the street. The boys followed him across the road, then through the supermarket parking lot, on to a pay phone just outside the doors.

Winslow lifted the receiver. He dropped in quarters, trying to ignore the boys behind him. But he couldn't think with them standing there, couldn't remember his old phone number. Someone tapped his shoulder. Winslow slammed down the receiver, spun to face them.

A grin flashed on the boy's round face. "Ten bucks says I can hurt you with a punch."

"This ain't the time, son."

The boy tugged his glove tight to his fist.

Winslow eyed him. As he turned back to the phone, the boy

slugged Winslow's kidney. A fuse was lit in him. He whirled and punched the boy stiff in the mouth.

The boy dropped to the walkway. Blood coated his teeth. The market door swung open and a bent old woman stood there gawking at the boy, at Winslow standing over him. Winslow sprinted away, his arms pumping, quarters tumbling from his pocket down onto the icy asphalt.

12

A thumping rattled the trailer door. Ham and Bently stood out in the freezing dark. Bently explained he had to put Winslow in jail, though he'd file no charges and knew those boys were bad news.

"Just so folks think I'm keeping order," the lawman said. "Don't have to stay in the cell. I'll even give you keys. Until the first of the year you just stick around the jail and don't let folks see you. Then you'll be free as a bird, with a new year and a clean slate."

Bently said Ham had something to tell him, too, and Ham stared into the cold trailer. "Goddamn, Red," he said, rubbing the flab of his neck. "No wild-man shows for a while. Until New Year's Eve, you got some time off from it."

Winslow nodded.

"Bently'll let you out to come to the house for Christmas, too," Ham said. "You're family to us, and we want you there."

Bently set a hand on Winslow's arm. "We're worried you'll get down around the holidays. You feel blue, you'll tell us, won't you?"

"I'm fine," Winslow said.

"We'll worry anyhow," the lawman said. "You just take it easy, friend. Get yourself back to center."

Winslow gave Ham a bottle of Scotch for Christmas. Now it was night, Christmas day come and gone, and Winslow poured a glass to empty the bottle. The family sat piled on the sofa across the room, Jim asleep, his head in his mother's lap, Sheila slumped against Ham, Ham with his drink balanced on his belly and his feet up on the coffee table.

It was quiet, very late, and Winslow asked, "Ever done something so bad folks won't forgive you?"

Sheila snuggled Ham's shoulder. "I got married."

Ham smirked. "Didn't use a rubber."

Wood popped in the chimney stove. Winslow watched the fire behind the grate. "I once met this fella who drove a train," he said. "A train just don't stop that fast. It just—" and Winslow gulped his Scotch, swallowed hard. "I mean, you ever stand by someone you can't forgive? Ain't no good saying, 'I forgive you.' Saying things don't do nothing. Not really." He held his glass to his cheek. "Just can't move away from myself."

Sheila's eyes opened, but she didn't move. Ham glanced down at Jim, ran a hand over the boy's head. "You oughtn't drink so much, Red," he said. "You don't do well with it."

Winslow downed his Scotch, scooted to the edge of his chair. "Thanks for Christmas."

"You going?" Ham asked, sounding surprised.

"Best get back to jail."

"You ain't in no shape to travel, Red."

Winslow stood. "I'll manage."

"You ain't gonna do nothing to yourself?" Ham said.

"Nah." Winslow leaned clumsily to set the glass on the coffee table. "Got a big show in a few days."

Winslow curled listless on his cot. All but the hours of Bently's visits, there he lay. He didn't exercise, didn't eat. Bently called in the doctor and Winslow claimed he just had a bug, said he'd be fine if they'd leave him to rest. The doctor gave him a bottle of pills. It was easy to dispose of them, to smash them beneath his heel and brush them away like so much dust. On the eve of New Year's Eve, his sentence coming to an end, Winslow donned a resolute face.

"Feel better today," he told Bently. "Doc fixed me up fine."

But Winslow had endured a disintegration of spirit. He no longer felt all he'd been through was a penance for what he'd done, a punishment to be served. Now this was just his life. He'd die in this skin, feeling this way.

Moonlight seeped through the high bars. Winslow thought of the train man whose path he'd followed months ago. He recalled the moon-white hair, the lips split by a scar. He could see the man racing through the barley, elbows high, growing smaller. Where did this man run to? Did his run ever end?

If you run, you run into nothing, Winslow decided, and he knew if he were to peer out that high cell window there'd be nothing, no road, no woods, just the black matter of space, and perched like a gargoyle atop the moon the train man would gaze down in judgment upon him.

13

The muzzle reeked of dung. "Ain't about you," Ham said, pressing the leather straps to Winslow's face, both men crammed in the tiny bathroom, the clamor from the bar thumping through the walls. "I'm thinking of the show. Any fool knows a wild man don't talk."

But Winslow knew it was about him, had always been about him. Ham buckled three straps at the back of Winslow's skull, and in the cloudy bathroom mirror his mouth cinched into a snarl.

"Goddamn, you look fierce," Ham said, smiling. "Sure as shit to get the big bucks tonight."

New Year's Eve and the bar was packed. Two men held a rope to keep the crowd at bay, and Winslow trailed Ham to the stage. Winslow wore only a strip of rawhide, wrists bound behind his back, stage lights in his eyes. Ham lifted the silver bell, but before he could ring it a commotion broke out, pushing, shoving, two men scuffling. Bently hurried into the throng and wedged himself between the brawlers. Winslow knew this was planned; Ham paid each man twenty dollars to fake a fight, claiming a riled crowd made better bids.

As Bently dragged the men through the rabble, Winslow saw him; a man with moon-white hair. Faces jostled, shouted. The lights were blinding. Hands bound, Winslow couldn't shield his eyes, couldn't find that face again. Ham rang the bell and hollered, *"The world has turned polite, some might say dainty—"*

Winslow peered frantically about for the train man. Fists flailed money, men shrieking bids. Ham helped a lanky man around the chicken wire. The man raised his fists like a fighter before the bell. The crowd wildly cheered. Winslow saw Ham ask him if he was ready, but could only hear the crowd.

Then he was there again, just beyond the fence, his scarred lips grinning. The train man's eyes burned into Winslow. He felt the guilt, the grief, all over again. The crowd shifted, like wind through barley, and the train man was gone.

Winslow lowered his eyes. He nodded to Ham, but left his abdomen limp.

The punch detonated deep inside Winslow. Without hands to break the fall, his face thudded against the floor. It was as if the world was suddenly without air, as if he were trying to scream but had no voice. Then the first bit of breath erupted into Winslow and he gasped beneath his muzzle.

Bottle shards rained over him. Men tore down the chicken wire.

Bently scrambled over Winslow, waving his pistol above his head. Pain burned through Winslow's side. He huffed through flared nostrils and, as if to stir himself from a nightmare, mumbled without ceasing, what once they removed the muzzle became a glut of painfully uttered words: *"Sadie. Call my Sadie—"*

14

Winslow woke to a figure in a sun-bright window, another moving toward him. This was a hospital. Pain throttled his side, bandages binding his ribs. One figure was a nurse, who made him swallow a pill with a glass of water. The other dragged a chair beside his bed. This was a law officer. He was muscular and had a child's face and wasn't Bently.

"You know why you're here?" the officer asked.

"My side hurts."

"Three broken ribs," he said. "Could've been worse."

Winslow blinked. "You close the drapes?"

"They say you asked to be hit?"

"Please."

"Say you got paid to be hit?"

Winslow raised a hand to shield his eyes.

"It was a show? That right?"

"The drapes. Please."

The nurse stepped to the window and closed the drapes. Winslow turned his cheek into his pillow. "A train hit me."

"What?" The officer leaned forward.

"A freight train."

The officer's hands were frail. He turned a wedding band on his thin finger. "Don't you want whoever did this to you to face due justice?"

Winslow shut his eyes. *"I did this."*

15

The nurse told Winslow he had a visitor. Winslow expected Bently or Ham. In walked Sadie. He studied her face, her silver cross, hair dyed the color of wheat, waiting for her eyes to prove she was real. She crossed the room and piled clothes on the chair by the window; his favorite green flannel shirt, jeans, his old brogans.

Then she turned and asked the nurse to see the doctor. He saw her eyes. It was really her. Winslow couldn't breathe. His body shook and electric pain tore through his ribs. He quietly moaned as Sadie, without a word, followed the nurse from the room.

Sadie remained in the hall while the nurse helped Winslow button his shirt, buckle his belt, tug on his boots. The nurse helped him into a wheelchair and pushed him out. Then Sadie took the nurse's place.

They rolled down a long tiled hall, Sadie silent behind him, and out into the parking lot. A gray sky hung low, the day unseasonably warm. Their truck sat in the far corner, out near the highway. In the field across the road, patches of soil showed through the snow. Beyond the field were hills dense with trees. The urge lingered to run into those woods, to hide away from the world.

Then they were at the truck. Sadie opened the door and Winslow climbed gingerly into the seat. He gazed out the windshield at the wintry hills. Sadie hardly glanced at Winslow. She covered him with a quilt as one might prepare a delicate piece of furniture for a long haul.

The truck descended a ramp to the interstate. They got up to speed and merged behind a semi. The wheels droned and the cab shook and Winslow tried to hold it down, but the pain and silence were too much. Tears ran hot down his face.

"Tell me if you need to stop," was all Sadie said.

They were the first words she'd spoken to him. Winslow swallowed to steady his voice. "How long a drive we got?"

"Five hours."

So long he'd walked, so much wandering, and now mere hours by truck. The land outside was open plains, the hills still in sight but fading, and though there was no quelling the pain in his side, Winslow leaned against the window and the glass cooled his face.

Rain ran down the windshield and the wipers thrummed. Winslow pretended to sleep, watched Sadie through his lashes. Her face was shadowed, but even through the darkness he believed he saw something altered in her face.

Sadie had never been able to lie to Winslow, her feelings always true in her eyes. From their first date in high school he'd teased she was incapable of keeping anything from him, and understood his ability to read her as a function of their love. Now he read nothing, and the place behind his sternum, what Winslow considered his heart, felt hollow with the possibility her face had nothing left for him.

He lolled his head and trained his eyes on the road. Brake lights flashed, a semi kicking mist. The wipers cleared the glass, but he could not see far enough beyond the road to know where they were.

They crossed the wide river, overflowing its banks, oil-black current churning through the boles of trees. The tires sang over the bridge. On the other side, Winslow read a billboard for the Chestertown Inn, where they'd stayed for their tenth anniversary. He remembered a featherbed and a room of sunshine and Sadie's sweet breath on his cheek.

"Got the hay harvested," Sadie said, the first either had spoken in hours. "Fred Halliday helped. Store paid pretty well." Set back from the road was a favorite restaurant of theirs, the Angus, a mammoth black steer on its roof. "Bought that old calico from William Bennet. The one Betty'd ride sometimes. It was a wild hair, but she's a good old horse."

Winslow wanted more words. Any words. Even the casual felt comforting. "How are William and Betty?"

"Alive," she said, and stiffened.

Old Saints Highway, Traverson Lane, Birch Road, Hickory, Mayapple: roads driven to school, to dates, roads mapped in memory. They'd taken the long way, avoiding the drive through town, and now cruised a straightaway, snow overfilling the ditches, then Sadie pumped the brakes and they crossed the freight tracks and there sat his home, high on the knob and blending with a gray-brown sky.

Snow covered everything, covered the tracks and hillside, drifts scaling the barn walls. A pack of whitetail does, undaunted by the truck turning into the drive, huddled in the near field, nibbling the wheat beneath the snow. If I'd been here during deer season, Winslow thought, them does wouldn't be out there. Now he'd have to ward them off, day after day, or they'd devour the crop. The truck slowed and then stopped by the house, the engine shut down and ticking.

"Need help inside?" Sadie asked, without looking at him. "Or you think you can make it alone?"

16

Her hair smelled as it'd always smelled, as she helped him down into the rocker. Then she was gone upstairs. The front parlor felt new, its wood paneling painted a pale yellow, and on the wall above the couch hung needlepoint, four rows of five pictures, each in simple white frames, threads brilliant in shades of reds and blues and oranges.

Sadie returned with his pajamas, sheets, a quilt, and a pillow. She made his bed on the couch. Then she crossed to the rocker and knelt before Winslow, helped him off with his boots. He wanted to kiss her hair, to pull her close. She helped him to the couch, handed him his pajamas, and left the room.

Winslow struggled changing alone, left his buttons undone, and climbed beneath the covers. He lay in lamplight, listening to a vacuum upstairs. The smell of pot roast filled the house. Then the vacuum stopped and Sadie came downstairs. He heard the oven door open, heard water from the faucet, plates clinking.

She brought in a plate and set it on the coffee table, handed him a glass of water, made him sit up and take his medicine. She told him to eat if he could. She said she'd see him in the morning. Then she was gone again, her footsteps ascending the stairs. Winslow stared at the plate until his eyes watered. With excruciating effort, he reached behind him and switched off the lamp.

17

Winslow lay awake, dwelling on all the people he'd soon face. The tragedy of a small town was that bygones never wholly dissipated; Winslow still held a grudge against William Gentry, who'd bullied him in grammar school, and could never see pure Annie Phillips, a registered nurse and mother of three, who as a girl skinny-dipped with the high school ball team. Winslow would prefer to get it over with, to stand in the Old Fox Tavern and let the entire town, one by one, slug him in his busted ribs.

But the grace of Krafton came with the seasons, sowing, reaping, breeding an understanding that last year has no bearing on this one; this crop might be better, or worse, and regardless there'll be another and then another. In this there was only the future and diligent work, and not emotion but movement, just as the rain falling or crops sprouting was not emotion.

Winslow decided he'd engage the forthcoming days in the movement of work, and tried to remember how his days had begun at this time last year. He imagined the farm taken to ruin, chickens unfed in their coop, cows bloated, the silo a high mash of seed gone to rot. He was tempted to dress and inspect the outbuildings. But his body wouldn't allow it.

Winslow managed to stand and carry a blanket to the rocker by the windows. The sky was clouded, the land black. He could see little beyond the yard, and told himself, as he had over years of taking crops to store, to allow last year's seed, which grew imperceptibly, day after day, and then was a stalk gone beneath the harvester reels, to vanish from his waking life, to be no more than a ghost in his dreams.

18

They drove along Elm Avenue. The town emerged from the fog, the diner on one side, the market across the road, their first-floor windows haloed in watery light. An old man in an orange parka, Marshall Traverson, stood beneath the diner's canopy and opened an umbrella over his wife, Leta. He raised a hand to the truck. Sadie returned Marshall's wave. Winslow shrank in his seat.

Soon came the Baptist church, nestled between barren fields. They parked at the end of the churchyard. Interior lights stoked color into the chapel's stained glass. Winslow didn't move. He watched silhouettes, vague behind the colored windows. Then Sadie opened his door. She offered a hand down and he took it and she helped him out.

Winslow lagged behind, studying cars in the lot, and in his mind he saw their owners inside, praying in the pews. An organ droned. A choir sang. Sadie was waiting up on the stoop and by the door, gripping the handle, eyeing him over her shoulder.

Winslow hesitated at the bottom step. He gazed out over the yard and beyond the field. Bleary through fog and distance stood a leafless line of trees. Choir voices swelled, as did Winslow's pulse, the woods so near and the voices rising higher, soaring, holding. Then all was quiet.

Winslow bolted into the churchyard. His heels slipped in the snow, each twist a knife to his ribs. Sadie shouted his name, but he didn't stop. He pushed past the church and into the field, dress shoes sloshing, sinking in the mud, eyes locked on the woods. Again Sadie hollered, shrill, desperate, a mother crying out to a lost child. Winslow stopped. He winced, gasping, his lungs burning.

Trees waved like dreams out in the mist. Sadie stood at the field's berm, hugging her Bible, watching him as one does a deer, something that may at any moment flee. Then Sadie herself ran with wild flight back through the yard, on around to the chapel doors.

Winslow blew into his fists. He shifted from shoe to shoe in the freezing mud. The chapel's windows opened. Faces appeared in the gaps. Men poured into the churchyard, and the pastor, a bull-shouldered man in a satin robe, hurried out into the field. He lifted his feet as if wading through a river, stepped close, and pulled Winslow into an embrace.

"Sure nice to see you, Win," he said. "A miracle. A true miracle." He rubbed his palms over Winslow's hands and bowed his head, and Winslow thought they might pray.

"Winslow?"

"Yes?"

"We've known each other too long for sidetalking," he said. "I'm not going to lie to you. It's not right for a man to run off like you did. Folks around here are awful sore at you."

Winslow nodded.

"But nobody's sore about what happened with your boy. Lord knows, it's not about that. You know it's not about that, right?"

Winslow's head felt full of mud. He couldn't lift his chin.

"Maybe we ought to get some coffee at Freelys?" the pastor said. "Can go tomorrow if you like? Introduce you around again?"

Winslow glanced off toward the snowy yard. A crowd milled in suits and dresses and choir robes. Sadie stood in the field now, mud splashed up her nylons.

The pastor set a hand on Winslow's collar. "The damned things I've seen in my years," he said, his eyes soft. "God gets around to all of us. Every last one of us. Who the hell knows what to do about it."

Winslow huffed and tried not to weep.

"Win." He pressed a palm to Winslow's cheek. "Even Christ needed time to hisself."

Winslow turned away from the hand.

"Even Christ needed time. Say it."

Winslow couldn't speak.

"Say it, Win."

"Even Christ—" was all he could get out.

The pastor's wingtips were up to the laces in mud. "Only fools stand out in a cold field. Fools and hunters." He grinned, smacked Winslow's shoulder. "Go on home, Win," he said, softly.

Winslow nodded.

He trailed Pastor Hamby through the mud. The pastor set his arm around Sadie, ushered her back into the churchyard. He called for everyone to get on inside, hollered that he hadn't even started preaching. Then Pastor Hamby lifted Sadie's hand and hooked it gently onto Winslow's arm. Sadie clutched Winslow's elbow, so intently, so fiercely, it hurt him though he dare not say.

19

Visitors came throughout the day. Winslow's cousins stopped by, his banker, his neighbors on both sides. They spoke of horse races and strip mines and coon dogs. Jimmy Lang got a six-point buck. Helen Farelley arrested Harlan Delmore for growing pot in his silo. Little Janice Franklin was pregnant again. Winslow lay on the couch, Sadie running to the kitchen for cookies and coffee. Nobody asked where he'd been, or how he'd gotten hurt, and Winslow guessed they already knew.

It felt like the funeral all over again, people talking cordially and hushed, bringing cakes and casseroles and jars of preserves. The mournful feel conjured in him an old buried memory, of a day Rodney had gone missing.

That evening had fallen dark, his boy lost since lunchtime. On the porch Sadie had held Winslow in her arms, telling him it'd be all right. Then they heard a horse bang its stall in the barn. They found Rodney asleep in a grain trough. In hindsight it was a precious vision, the child curled as if in a womb. But Winslow had yanked him up by his arm, screaming all the dreadful things that happen to a child left on his own. Sadie had taken Winslow's hand and led him to the house, telling him his mind had made it bigger than it was. She'd let Rodney lag behind.

Winslow remembered that clearly now, remembered it as he never had before, and realized Sadie always knew he, even more than Rodney, needed close watching over, needed her steady comfort and good sense.

————————

The house was lightless in all but the parlor. Sadie served him a bowl of tuna casserole, said she was worn out. "I'm going to take a bath and get to bed," she told him, her eyes on the foyer staircase. "You take your pill and get the lights off?"

"Of course," Winslow said, from the couch.

"Watch the TV if you like." She stepped into the foyer. "Don't stay up too late."

"Sadie?"

"Remote's on the table." She held the banister, gazed up the dark stairs.

"Sadie?"

She turned just her head. Sadie's eyes found his, and they saw each other. "I wish I could take my brain and put it inside your head," Winslow said. "Just for a moment. Then you'd know what all I can't find how to say."

Sadie grinned, her eyes weary. "Sleep well, Winslow," she said. "See you in the morning."

20

Winslow couldn't sleep. He gazed at the pictures above the couch, colors bleeding in the dark, though gold doves shone bright in one, a pink bull in another. Winslow strained to the edge of the couch. The floor was cold. He walked into the foyer. Framed needlepoint hung where photos of Rodney once had. Winslow mounted the stairs and ran his fingers over the thread; a silver bear with its paw in a blue bee's nest, a green girl skipping rope, a red sailboat in a sea of black.

He crossed to his old bedroom. The bed was empty, unrumpled. Sadie was not there. Winslow turned back into the hall. Rodney's door was opened a crack, a line of light across the floor. He tread softly down, the light passing over his foot, then up his leg. Winslow set his ear to the door. With the tips of his fingers, he eased it open.

The sky outside had lightened, the room washed in a metallic sheen. Football pennants plastered the walls. A child's desk filled one corner, messy with model cars, a dirty dinner plate, Ball jars furred with dust. In the other corner, beneath the room's only window, stretched a twin bed. There Sadie slept, the covers drawn to her chin.

Winslow stepped to the window. The sky hung green. Soon it would snow. The hillside of winter wheat lay swaddled in snow, the rails of freight tracks like silver spears over the wet road.

He glanced down at Sadie. Hair fell loose across her mouth. Her eyes were open, staring up at him.

Winslow held his side and lowered himself to the floor. He rested his cheek on the mattress. Her eyes stayed on him. Slowly her hand emerged from the covers. She brushed the hair from her lips. Those same fingers reached across the mattress. Winslow closed his eyes. He nuzzled her hand. She didn't pull away.

Winslow felt her edge nearer, felt her over him, her hair brushing his ear, his chin. Her breath blew warm on his face, as she whispered, "Your hair has turned so white."

SMOKE

A voice called his name. Vernon woke to the haze of dawn, and a figure slouched in through the open window beside his bed. Vernon was hungover. His eyes pulsed and he rubbed them to clear his vision. The figure raised erect, balanced itself with one hand on the sill. Beyond, the pastel sky blazed.

"Vernon," the voice said again.

"Pop?"

"Couldn't make it alone, son."

Vernon sat up and dropped his legs off the bed.

"Wear them old boots," his father said. "Them new ones ain't broke in yet."

His father wore a filthy undershirt, his hand swaddled in a blood-stained rag. A cut sliced the meat of his shoulder, the skin jaggedly sewn with green thread. With his good hand he pulled a comb from his back pocket and dragged perfect lines through his oiled hair.

Then he returned the comb to his pocket and rested his head against the window frame.

"Don't wake your mama," he whispered, and took Vernon's hand. "Wear them old boots, son. It's a ways we got to go."

Vernon stepped in bare feet out the front door. The humid air poured over him. He stuck his feet in his old boots and walked off the porch and on around the side of the house where his father sat on a soda crate beneath his bedroom window. His father's eyes were closed. In his right hand he clutched a gunnysack.

"Pop?"

His father's eyes opened but he did not stir. "I'm sorry, Vernon," he said. "A son shouldn't have to see his father this way."

"I don't feel good, neither."

"That don't say much for the both of us," he said. "Now help me up and keep quiet."

At fifteen, Vernon was already taller and broader than his father. He reached around his father's waist, as if hugging a tree, and lifted. "No, no," his father groaned, and slumped to one side, and Vernon knew he'd tugged the stitches on his shoulder. His father held his injured hand in the air. He slowly braced a knee beneath himself and stood without assistance. Vernon tried to take the gunny, but his father yanked it away. Then, with an overtired sigh, his father offered Vernon the gunnysack.

It was heavier than Vernon expected. Inside was a thick coil of rope and a tire iron, and he could not figure what they'd be used for. Then his father was pushing through the sweetbriar and entering the shade of the woods.

"Where we going?" Vernon asked.

His father didn't answer, but descended a gentle slope, bracing himself against saplings to slow his momentum. Vernon caught up quickly and found he had to pause between steps to stay beside his father. Halfway down, his father leaned against the mossy trunk of an oak tree. He shivered, his elbows clamped to his ribs. Then he pushed off the tree and straightened himself.

"I've been up all night and I want to tell you some things," he said. "But not here. Let's get there first. I ain't very strong and we just need to get there." He reached back his good hand and Vernon took it. "Your mama sewed me up. She won't never see me the same. Once things change they don't never turn back."

His father's voice scared Vernon and he held his father's hand and helped him down the hill.

"Wouldn't you be better in your bed?" Vernon asked.

"They'd find me in my bed."

Vernon wondered who *they* were, wondered where his father was leading him. It was rare for them to hike off into the east. There used to be a couple of families in these woods, but their wells ran dry and they had to move closer to town. Vernon pretended they were going to check the coon traps. Maybe Pop couldn't reset them traps with his hand busted up, he told himself, though he knew it was a lie.

Vernon followed his father through swales of prickly weeds and honey locust. His skull felt as if filled with thistle; the Nordgren brothers had stolen three fifths of whiskey from the Old Fox, and Vernon finished an entire one himself during last night's double feature at the picture show. The sun burst full over the hilltops and Vernon wanted to keep walking to get to where they were going, but then he had to piss and asked his father if they could stop. His father said nothing, but eased himself down on a stump. Vernon unhooked his overalls and peed over the wilted bells of cardinal flowers. When he turned around his father had fallen backward, his legs drooped over the stump. Vernon ran and propped him up. His father's skin was the pale gray of something extinguished.

"Are you my daddy?" his father said up to Vernon.

"You all right, Pop?"

A queer smile brightened his father's face. "You remember when I came home from the war?"

They'd had a party and a cake with lemon icing. "Yes, sir."

"Remember the first thing you said to me?"

"No, sir."

"You was so small, just a tiny child, and you stood like a soldier in the doorway and looked up and asked, 'Are you my daddy?'"

His father's eyes were far off, were black dots beneath papery lids. "I met you at the bus," Vernon said, like breaking bad news. "Weren't but a year ago. I was tall as you. You said, 'You're a mirror to me,' and you had me try on your coat and it fit me just right."

His father gazed up at him, and his eyes seemed to suddenly take focus. "That's right," he said. "That was *me* who said that. That was me and my pop."

His good hand gripped Vernon's arm, and he took his feet and stumbled over the stump and found his stride. Vernon followed behind his shoulder. If his father wobbled even slightly, Vernon grabbed his belt and pulled him straight.

After they had walked several miles, the low hills rose into steep striated limestone and the ground became slanting flats of rock. His father stepped off to where in past years flowed a trickle of waterfall, but was now a dry basin stained a powdery white. Vernon followed his father across the basin, on around an outcropping guarding a dry streambed. In the rock's shade something large was wrapped in his parents' bedspread, a blue and red bearpaw quilt. For a moment Vernon thought his father had shot a deer out of season. Then he noticed an uncovered shoe; a patent leather oxford, its wax lace untied. His father knelt and waved away flies with his good hand, then gently set his hand atop the quilt.

"I killed this man," he said. "I wish I hadn't, but I did."

Vernon struggled to know what to say. He stared at the shoe and kept expecting it to twitch. He became mindful that he'd been made part of a big secret, an ugly secret.

"Who is he?"

"Don't really know," his father said. "Name's Nory Augusto. Learned that from his wallet."

"What you kill him for?"

His father pulled the quilt to cover the shoe. "We best get him hid," he said. "Took all night to drag him this far. Couldn't get him over the rocks myself. He ain't that big a man. You ought to be able to heft him all right."

Vernon gazed nervously about at the sunlight. Through all his adventures of hunting arrowheads in these woods he'd never crossed paths with another human. Still he glanced above at the shadow-strewn crest of the rock, then at the slashes of tree trunks down in the hollow and into the canopy where the sun flashed off leaves as it might off a lawman's spectacles or the buckle of a holster.

Vernon quickly grabbed two fistfuls of quilt. He set his legs and hoisted the body across his neck and shoulders, as if he were carrying a calf. The quilt smelled of his mother's detergent. Then a second odor seeped out, something like urine and musk cologne. Vernon gagged but kept hold. He steadied himself, then followed his father around a flat rock.

As Vernon stepped up large slabs, his father pressed a firm hand on the body to keep him from tumbling backward. At the bluff's ridge, Vernon was exhausted and his head throbbed and he could feel the man's hip bones on his neck. He leaned into the shade of a cliff and vomited. Whiskey and chocolate silk pie came up, and the smell of it made him retch again. Bile stung sour on his gums. He wished he had water to rinse his mouth. His father did not say a word, but wiped his eyes with a handkerchief and turned away.

Vernon had never seen his father cry. This overwhelmed him and he began to cry, too, and his father continued to cry and Vernon found that weeping made his head feel better. They did not look at each other or speak as they trod the jagged downslope weeping.

They pushed through a prairie of broom sedge. This was farther than Vernon had ever been to the east. The white sun was unbearable and he wished he'd worn a hat. He marched like a mule, one foot in front of the other, slow and steady. They hiked half an hour through the high stiff grass, pausing several times for Vernon to rest, before they again entered the shade of the woods, and ten minutes more before they came upon a rock jutting from the earth like a giant blunted tooth. Vernon followed his father's eyes up the sandstone slope to a ledge fifty feet up. His father reached into the gunnysack and removed the rope and shook it loose from its coil.

"Put a log beneath Mr. Augusto," his father said. "Tie this rope up around his knees and chest."

"What we gonna do?"

"Climb."

Vernon found a log as thick as his leg and turned the quilt and body belly-up over it. He secured the ropes. His father tied the rope around his waist, with plenty of slack left atop the body. Vernon cinched the loose end of the rope around his own waist.

"Take it slow," his father said, and gave Vernon the tire iron in the gunnysack. "If you can get up there carrying that gunny, then I surely can with my hand busted."

"What's up there?"

His father peered up at the ledge. "A cave. I been in it before. It's a good cave. Nobody much knows of it."

The rock was steep, but pocked with footholds. Vernon moved slowly, trying not to crumble the soft rock, glancing down between his legs to gauge his father's progress.

They found their way high up the rock face. At the precipice, Vernon threw over the gunny and scurried onto the ledge and pulled the rope tight. His lungs heaved. Sweat stung scrapes where his chin had rubbed the rock. His father came slowly behind, his face and chest yellow with sandstone chalk, and moaned as he crawled onto the ledge. They lay side by side on the hot rock. The summit loomed high above the ledge, baking in the full sunlight.

"I killed Mr. Augusto with that tire iron," his father said.

Vernon lay on his back, breathing hard, and watched his father's swaddled hand tremble atop the rope around his waist. His father rose. "Come on," he said. "Let's pull him up."

At the edge of the cliff, Vernon took up the slack of rope. He was afraid to look down into the woods for fear he'd see someone and someone would see him. He flexed his grip and leaned backward, taking tiny steps. The body's heft took anchor, then Vernon dug in his heels and each step was a harried thrust. His father did what he could, pulling with his good hand, and they continued backward until they'd run out of cliff and were against the rock wall. Then, fist over fist, Vernon advanced to the edge and muscled the body up a few more feet. In this fashion the body in the quilt was soon on the ledge.

His father told him to untie Mr. Augusto and so he did. Vernon and his father remained belted with the rope, and as Vernon knelt over the body the rope tugged him toward where his father had disappeared into a gap in the rock face.

Vernon quickly followed. The rope stayed taut between them and

Vernon stepped into the gap. The air turned cool and damp. Sunlight fell through a fissure high overhead and striped the sloping white-rock tunnel. Vernon shuffled down and watched darkness rise like water up his father's back and then he was gone.

The light dwindled for Vernon. He felt along the wall with his fingertips. In his other fist the tire iron in the gunnysack swung freely. He clanked the sack against a wall and rock crumbled away. He struck the tunnel again, this time with purpose, and sizable chunks dropped onto his boots. Vernon stepped down through the darkness, wondering if it was easy to kill a man with a tire iron.

Bright light bloomed as the tunnel abruptly turned, and Vernon crawled through a narrow chute to enter a stalactite cavern. The center of the cathedral roof had eroded into a natural and perfect oval. Blazing sun poured through the oval. The walls and floor shone like polished pearl. His father sat on a slab of gray stone, one of three slabs among all that wet glowing calcite. The rope lay on the ground at his father's feet, and Vernon untied his end and let it drop.

"What is this place?"

"The Indians used it, I think," his father said. "Someone put these benches in here."

Vernon sat on a slab and hugged himself. The sweat from the climb had soaked his clothes and now gave him a chill.

"I want you to know me as I am, Vernon," his father said. "I don't want you to see me as good no more. A man what kills someone ain't no good." His father leaned against the damp wall and studied the sky. "You remember that long road we took to get to the Miller rigs? That long dirt road that went on forever?"

"Yes, sir," Vernon said, and he remembered driving an hour on a thin dirt road. He remembered nothing but oil pumps and flat fields and a horizon that didn't buckle.

"Another truck come along that road yesterday. Seven years I ain't never seen a soul on that road, and here comes some shiny truck like it ain't never been dirty. And you know how steep them ditches are. Well, me and Mr. Augusto come nose to nose with our trucks. Don't know who built that road. Don't know what kind of a man makes a road ain't wide enough for two trucks to pass. Surely weren't Christian, whoever he was."

His father ran his good hand through his hair, resting his palm against his forehead. "Mr. Augusto weren't backing up for nobody," he said. "Ain't never seen the man in my life and told him he didn't have no right on that road, how it was company land and how I was the foreman and he should just back on up before I had him put away for trespassing. I know you been in fights, Vernon. I don't keep my head buried like you might think. You know fighting's a bad thing?"

"I guess."

"It is, Vernon," his father said. "But when two men don't agree, then they's nothing left. We could talk in circles for days and them trucks'd still be nose to nose. I had that tire iron just for show. Before I knew it he had a knife on me and cut me bad. And then something come up in me and I hit Mr. Augusto across his skull. He fell like someone switched him off. Weren't but one hit. I thought a great deal about it last night. When a fire goes out there's a smoldering and a little smoke left to trail. This man weren't snuffed like a fire. I switched him off like a houselight, and it don't seem right."

Vernon thought of the homes in town with electricity, of the diner and picture show, of how their windows glowed in the dark night.

"I wonder where he was heading?"

"I wonder about that, too," his father said. "I've sure been wondering about a lot of things. I wonder if Mr. Augusto has a wife and children. Ain't no photos in his wallet, but ain't none in mine neither."

His father filled his lungs and exhaled and closed his eyes. "I wonder if Hell is real," he said. "You think Hell is real?"

It wasn't a question Vernon had ever studied. "I don't know."

"I've been thinking a great deal about Hell. I don't want to go there. I don't know if it's a real place or not, but a man can't take his chances."

"You ought to lay on that bench over there, Pop. It's in the sun a little. You oughtn't stay in the shade with those wounds."

"I been thinking about Jesus, too. I figure Jesus wouldn't have got nowhere if he were always backing down a road. Even Jesus had to stand and take his licks."

"That man stabbed you," Vernon said. "He might've killed you."

"He's got a name. Don't call him *that man*," his father said, and opened his eyes and rose and walked to the dry bench in the sun. "Mr. Augusto surely weren't going to back down. But he weren't no different than me." He lay back on the bench and covered his eyes with his arm. "Vernon?"

"Yes, sir?"

"You know why I believe there's a God?"

"No, sir."

"I feel a powerful tenderness for Mr. Augusto. Don't make no sense otherwise. A man what come after me. A man I don't know from Adam. Yet I'm still very sorry for him. If you wronged someone and still want to do good by them, I believe that tenderness is God up in you. I feel more tenderness for Mr. Nory Augusto than any man alive. I believe God is full up in me."

"Maybe the Devil was in you when you did it?"

"I don't know," he said. "What's better anyway, Vernon? To have the Devil in me, or to have it be me alone?"

"You ain't a bad man, Pop."

His father shook his head. "We are what we do."

"You ain't bad. I believe in that."

"No, Vernon," his father said. "I'm about as bad as they come. Now go on and bring Mr. Augusto in here. I need to lay still and be quiet awhile."

"Mr. Augusto would've killed you."

"Then he'd be the bad man," his father said, quietly. "Now leave me be awhile, Vernon. Gather wood for a fire. We'll need lots of wood."

Vernon studied his father in the milky light, searching for something in his face, or the way he held his body, that was evidence of the good man he knew as a child. If God didn't want Mr. Augusto dead, why'd he let Pop kill him? With all the killing in the world, did one more man really matter?

Vernon crossed the room and crawled from the shimmering cavern. Maybe awful things is how God speaks to us, Vernon thought, trudging up the lightless tunnel. Maybe folks don't trust in good things no more. Maybe awful things is all God's got to remind us he's alive. Maybe war is God come to life in men. Vernon pushed on toward the light of day. He stepped out onto the ledge and into the heat, and it felt like leaving a theater after the matinee had shown a sad film, the glare of sunshine after the darkness far too real to suffer.

From the ledge, Vernon could see for miles: knobs of redbuds, poplars, dogwoods. The sky was slashed with smoke. Two thick black columns to the north, what Vernon figured was from the foundry stacks. An airy gossamer of soot far to the south, from coal barges out on the river. A curl of black smoke hung in the distant blue to the west, what Vernon knew was from town. It'd been a hot summer, with many fires; the bowling alley had burned to cinders, as had

Prentice Baldwin's house on the edge of town, the Harroget dairy, a grain silo out by the quarry. Vernon wondered what in town was on fire this time. The woods below had been slapped by drought but were still generally green. In the heart of this green was a circle of bare-branched hickories, leafless as they might look in winter.

Vernon climbed carefully down the cliff and began gathering wood. His eyes were parched knots, and his stomach churned. He strolled the forest looking for fruit trees, but could only find a sun-blanched spread of brambles with a palmful of rock-hard berries. Vernon sucked sourness from seed and pulp, and surveyed the forest floor for more. He saw none and moved on, hunting out anything edible, dead or alive, and trod like an Indian through the fern, trying not to rustle the leaves or make a sound, and imagined himself a boy-shaped breeze drifting above the earth.

Soon he was inside the circle of barren hickories he'd seen from the cliff. The dirt was cragged. The trees were the color of ashes. Limbs like bones stretched into each other. The air smelled of fire, and Vernon noticed threads of smoke leaked from the flayed bark of several trunks. As he collected kindling, a deep hopelessness came over him. He stared at the sky, at heat waves rippling from the tips of black branches. It felt to Vernon as if a bomb had been dropped here.

He sat in the shade beside a smoldering trunk. In a waking dream he imagined the approach of whistling through the woods. The whistled tune grew closer, then out rode a man in a white cowboy hat atop a golden, white-faced horse. It was Roy Rogers on Trigger, exactly as Vernon remembered them from the movie he'd seen the night before. They stopped in front of Vernon, towered over him. Roy wore a pale-blue shirt and a tomato-red neckerchief, his pants tucked inside his boots.

Roy leaned over the saddle horn, tipped his hat. "Hey, Vernon."

"Hey, Roy," Vernon said. "She's a hot one, ain't she?"

Roy glanced about the stand of trees. "It's like bull's breath out here." He dismounted, patted Trigger's flank, and looped the reins over a low branch. He stretched his back, then sat on his heels in front of Vernon and broke a twig into small pieces, tossing them off into a patch of chickweed. Vernon saw him glance at his old boots patched with rawhide and wire, then Roy's eyes lit a pained expression. "You want to sing a song, Vernon?"

"Nah."

"Ain't nobody around but us."

"I ain't got no voice for singing them dumb songs."

Roy's brows pinched together. "My songs ain't dumb, Vernon. You got a problem with my songs, you got a problem with me."

"Nothing against you, Roy. I just don't see why you got to pull a guitar from behind a cactus bush every five minutes."

Roy snapped the twig, chucked it aside. "I don't see a damn thing wrong with it," he said, pulling his gloves tight over his knuckles. "People like it just fine, if you ask me. Maybe you ought to give it a try before making slanderous remarks."

"I just think I'd feel dumb singing them songs."

"God damn it, kid," Roy said, and balled a fist in Vernon's face. "I ain't fooling with you. You sing or I'll bust your teeth."

"Hey," Vernon said. "What's the matter with you, Roy?"

Roy breathed hotly, in and out. His eyes were dark like small burnt twigs. Then he looked away, spat, and backed off.

Roy sat against the tree beside Vernon and gazed down at his hands. "Geez, I'm sure sorry," he said. "They've been putting me through some tough times lately. I know it's my job and is what it is, but damn it, what with the war and so much fighting I just need to be out on a lonesome plain with me and Trigger and nobody around for a hundred miles."

"Them boys did lock you in that freezer a couple pictures back,"

Vernon said in a comforting way. "And that one gal sent them wild dogs after you, too. Boy, was she some piece of work."

"Folks think it's easy because I sing a few songs and have a friendly disposition, but they don't know how hard it is."

"I know, Roy. I know what it's like."

"You're a good friend, Vernon. A good man."

They fell silent and Trigger swatted flies with his tail, and Roy held the bridge of his nose with two gloved fingers. "I sure need to sing," he said. "Won't you sing with me? Ain't nobody around but us."

Then Vernon was crying, and wiped his nose on the back of his hand. "Roy?"

"Yes, Vernon?"

"I hardly know him," Vernon said. "I hardly know my own father since he come home. I know you better than my own father."

"Every boy in America knows me better than their father," Roy said, and patted Vernon's knee. "That's why they love me so. Now what say we sing that song?"

"I ain't like you, Roy," Vernon said, sobbing. "I'm shit scared all the time. I'm just a rope of sand. What if the war starts up again, Roy? It will sometime, won't it? Folks say it will. I don't want to end up like him. Don't want to kill nobody. What if I got to take my turn?"

"You ain't any different than me, Vernon," Roy said. "I just sing a song every now and again to take off the dark edges. What say we sing one now? Just to smooth off the dark edges?"

Vernon wiped his eyes on his arm. "All right then."

Vernon stood and squeezed the bundle of sticks on his shoulder and ambled off through the forest, singing what words he could recall from "Get Along, Little Doggies." He took his time, gathering more wood as he went, and soon was back at the honeycomb rock.

He stopped singing and tied the bundle and began to climb, the song gone and the rocks so hot he had to spit on his palms to keep them from burning.

The body lay on the ledge in the summit's long shadow. Vernon stood over it with the sticks on his shoulder. He nudged the quilt edge with the toe of his boot. A corner folded over and revealed an ear and dark hair salted white and a cheek as smooth as ivory. That skin flustered Vernon. He lifted more quilt with his boot. A green eye showed itself, staring into nothing. Vernon had to see the rest of Mr. Augusto. He pulled a stick from his bundle and threw the quilt open.

The man was thin and wore gray trousers pressed with a hard crease. He wore a matching vest with brass buttons, and a shirt the color of a salmon fillet. He looked like a politician. Like a preacher. The left side of his face was unscathed. The right eye socket was a blood-crusted pit, the cheekbone collapsed, and a gash ran from his forehead down the side of his nose to the point of his chin.

Vernon turned over the boulder to be sick, but there was nothing left inside him. He ran into the cool of the tunnel. Slumped against the wall, he steadied his breathing. Then Vernon descended through strata of pallid light and tried to imagine this man wielding a knife. But he could not rectify the image in his mind and the pristine brass buttons and clean-shaven face.

He entered the cavern to find his father asleep and shivering on the sun-washed granite slab. His father's hand was unwrapped from its swaddling. Green stitches closed a gash on the back of his hand. His fingers were gnarled and black. Red blisters made a gross topography across his palm and wrist.

Sunlight streamed a harsh tide into the cathedral, and water trickling down the walls threw tiny prisms. Vernon set his load of wood in the center of the benches. He lightly shook his father's arm. His father's eyes opened enough to show white through his lashes.

"I need your lighter, Pop."

His father's eyes batted, closed again. Vernon dug into his father's pant's pocket and found the silver lighter.

The damp air made the fire difficult to start. Soon the wood crackled and let off a thin roil of smoke. His father now sat in a slouch, trying to comb his hair with a quivering hand. Vernon took the comb from him and ran it carefully through his father's hair.

"You was shivering." Vernon gave his father the comb. "They's lots of fires around. Don't think ours'll draw notice."

His father nodded. "Thank you, Vernon," he said. "Now bring Mr. Augusto in here, please. And plenty more wood. Several big logs. Use the rope to get them up here if need be."

Vernon found he could no longer look at his father, and just did as told. He exited the cave and to keep his mind off unpleasantness tried to focus on each singular movement: putting his foot in a pock of sandstone, breaking down sticks, piling them on his shoulder, stepping through fern, dragging thick sections of birch he found not far from the rock, and up the cliff, back down, feet moving, hands on hot rocks, stacking logs high on the burgeoning fire.

He dragged the quilt down the calcite corridor, Mr. Augusto's head knocking against the damp floor. Vernon pulled tenderly, as if dragging a man asleep and trying not to wake him. He became intensely aware of his own skin, the cloth on his fingertips, blisters crinkling the balls of his feet. Soon he felt heat from the fire on his neck, and he tugged the body, as if entering a furnace, through the cavern's mouth.

The fire lashed flames the size of small trees and the oval of blue sky was overcome by the smoke and the cathedral walls now reflected firelight instead of sunshine. His father approached and they stood with the body in the quilt between them.

"Help get it on the fire, son."

"You mean Mr. Augusto?"

"That's right," and his father solemnly nodded. "Help get Mr. Augusto on the fire. We got to burn him up."

Vernon stood very still. "I know you hit Mr. Augusto more than one time," he said. "You says you hit him only once, but that ain't the truth."

His father covered his mouth with his good hand. "Took one hit to switch him off," he finally said. "Just like I says. But then I was more mad with him dead than when he was alive."

His father straddled the quilt, struggled lifting Mr. Augusto's feet with his one hand, and Vernon grabbed the quilt up under the shoulders. They awkwardly dropped the body and the fire was momentarily smothered and the break in the smoke brought a flash of bright light. Then the sun was gone again and the flames grew livid as his father stirred the logs. Vernon sat on a granite bench, covering his nose to the smoke and facing his shadow flickering on the wall.

"Vernon," his father said, standing at his shoulder. "I want you to take your mama out tonight." He handed Vernon a folded wad of dollars. "Get her a nice steak. Take her to the picture show." He sat down beside Vernon, cradling his black-fingered hand tight to his ribs. "When you come back home tonight, Mama'll go and meet me at the old McAlester Road. From there we're gone."

Vernon wondered if the money his father had given him was from Mr. Augusto's wallet, and allowed himself to peek behind at the fire. His eyes blinked against the heat, the quilt fabric burned away in spots to expose the body. Mr. Augusto's arm stretched to the edge of one bench, his shirt cuff wriggling with fire yet the hand untouched, the flames reflecting hard off his gold watch. Waves of smoke scorched Vernon's eyes. He turned back to the wall. His father had slumped forward, as if poised to be sick.

"You're going to die, ain't you, Pop?"

His father raised himself straight. "Maybe I am. I don't know. I just got to get to somewhere I can get my hand worked on and nobody'll ask questions."

"I'll go with you."

"No."

"I got to."

His father watched smoke billow black into the sky, then leaned into Vernon. "Listen to me, son," he said. "I been thinking on what to do with you, and I want you to listen close." Vernon wiped his stinging eyes, tried to focus on his father's mouth. "Tomorrow," his father said, "I want you to pack your belongings into a bag and walk yourself into town to the Baptist church. Go on to Pastor Gould and tell him everything. Tell him how I killed a man. How you had to carry the body. How I made you help burn him up. Tell him you need the Lord. They can't turn you away; you're fruit to be picked or go rotten. You go it straight, son, and they'll give you a life. You'll be a symbol to them, of how someone can come out of the fire and become righteous. You'll be a symbol and they'll take good care of you always 'cause folks need something to believe in. I'll be a symbol, too."

Then he was quiet and draped his good arm around Vernon's shoulders. His head lolled, then Vernon was looking into his father's gray eyes. "This thing we done, Vernon," he said. "It's outside of so much. I've worried about all the things that'll change. But I been thinking about them things what can't be touched. Ain't a woman in the world more beautiful than your mother. I was thinking about how much I loved her, and how that ain't changed, and that got me think-

ing about my heart and how when it rains your skin and hair gets wet
and cold, but your heart don't know if it's raining, or hot, or windy. It
just keeps on beating." He lifted his arm back from around Vernon.
"That's how I like to think about it, at least. It ain't all clear in my
mind yet." He motioned toward the cave entrance. "Go on, now. Take
your mother out tonight and try and just forget about me."

In a gesture they'd often shared when Vernon was a child, his father kissed his cheek. Vernon touched his father's hair, then rose and
did not look back. He was barely conscious of his movement as he
wandered up and out from the tunnels.

He mindlessly negotiated the sandstone facade. He walked the
woods thinking he should climb back to the cave, that there was
more to be said, that he should stay and help his father. But the
ground passed quickly beneath him and he did not slow until wire
patching his boot soles snagged the grass of the dense sedge prairie.

Vernon turned to face what was behind him. Above the tree line
rose the smoking sandstone peak. Black smoke smeared the sky like
an oily thumb dragged down pretty paper. In that smoke were brass
buttons and blood. Vernon's eyes burned from smoke. His hands and
arms were beaded with soot-black sweat. Smoke clung to his hair,
his clothes, his skin. He tasted smoke on his teeth.

Flames flared behind Vernon's breastbone. He coughed and he
spat and wheezed. He became light-headed. He dropped to one
knee. Sedge swayed in his eyes and he could no longer see the peak.
He saw only smoke-hazed sky. The sky had been sullied for so long
Vernon couldn't recall a day without smoke. He lay on his back in the
grass, but could not quell the heat in his chest. Wind-blown smoke
swirled in the sky above where he lay, higher, swirling higher, and
though he longed to believe his father, to understand him, he knew
smoke was not rain and had found its way to his heart.

He watched the sky and thought of all the fires the world had ever seen, fires from wars, fires from bombs. So much smoke. Where has it all gone? New smoke curled beneath wisps of old, drifting ever higher, higher. Where does it all go? He inhaled deeply and his insides burned, and Vernon knew all that smoke was now just the air we breathe.

PEACEKEEPER

Spring 2008: There were more direct routes to the Odd Fellows Hall, on a dry knob north of town, but Helen Farraley could not see below the muddy floodwater, couldn't risk wrecking the boat on a tree or chimney or telephone pole. Who knew what was just below the surface? The streets of town were lined with ancient oaks, the leafy tops of which stuck out from the water like massive shrubs. Helen steered the boat through the channel between them. The others in the boat sat silent as they passed their neighbors' homes, slate-shingled Victorians under water to the second-floor windows. Helen trolled high above the town's main street, Old Saints Road, and the treetops dropped away as the land sloped into the valley's low.

They passed the SuperAmerica gas station, only the hump and peak of the SA on its road sign visible. The others stared into the muck water as if they might see the pumps or store below. Afloat in the current were random lumber, tree branches and strips of siding, a pair of trundling bar stools, a long metal box Helen believed was either a school locker or a feed trough. Then came Freely's Diner and Freely's General, three-story brownstones on opposite sides of the road, water up to the white-stone facing, roofs like rectangular docks. They passed within arm's distance of the electric sign that read FREELY'S, which usually shone bright red, but was now dark and hung just above the waterline. Freda Lawson, who wore a chambray dress over yellow waders and sat beside Helen, ran a finger along the sign's second E. Helen yanked down the woman's arm.

"There's wires," she snapped. Then she gently held Freda's elbow, and softened. "Please be careful, hon."

They passed high above the converted boxcar that was the Old Fox Tavern, and the First Baptist Church, its steeple jutting crooked from the water like the mast of a sunken ship.

"They'll steal everything we got," Jake Tiernen said from the bow, his wife beneath his arm. "They'll take what all they want."

Freda twisted the hem of her dress around her fist. "I wet myself," she whispered to Helen, crying.

"Ain't nobody stealing nothing," Helen said, and leaned a shoulder into Freda to let her know she'd been heard.

"The hell," Jake said. "The hell they won't."

Christmas Eve, 2007: Light from Freely's Diner spilled over the snowy walkway and into the cruiser. Helen checked her face in the rearview mirror. Her left eye was badly swollen, and she tried to hide it by tilting her cap over her brow. She considered driving on. But then Freely stood in the diner's window, the old man thin and hunched and his hands cupped against the glass. Helen climbed out into the cold. She walked around the car and Freely moved to the door and opened it a crack. "I got pecan pie," the old man said through the crack, then Helen was at the door and he opened it wide.

Helen stepped in and Freely had his arms around her in a hug. Ten years she'd worked in Freely's General before becoming Krafton's first and only law officer. It'd been Freely, longtime mayor of Krafton, who decided any real town had a sheriff, and raised funds to buy an old cruiser from the Boonville force, and called a town meeting in the First Baptist Church. It'd been a joke that Helen, a middle-aged grocery store manager, had been nominated and then elected, and when protests arose—*I thought it'd be a goof to vote for her, didn't think she'd win*—it was Freely who declared civilized democracies stuck by a vote.

The dinner crowd had just left. Ham and potatoes fragranced the air. "I ain't hungry," Helen said. "Just saw the lights on."

"No, no," the old man said, hustling behind a glass counter. He pulled one of two pies from the dessert case and put the pie in a box. "You coming for Christmas supper? Marilyn said you might."

Helen studied the front window. Jocey Dempsy's photo was in all the shopwindows; her middle-school portrait, a ponytail tied with red ribbon, braces, a blemish on her hawk nose. MISSING across the top. REWARD across the bottom. "Don't know," Helen said.

The old man was in front of her again. He held the box with the pie inside and wore a fur-lined coat that was much too large for him. "What you done to your eye?"

Helen turned toward the door. "Slipped on some ice."

"Clumsy girl," and he took her arm. "Walk me home?"

They left out onto the walkway. Freely's hand shook and he struggled to put the key in the lock. His house was down the road and up a small hill. Warm light shone from the windows, colored lights twined around two large spruce by the porch steps. "Looky there," he said, pointing across the road. Over the dark field colored sparks burst, rained, faded in the night sky. They sounded far away, maybe miles, the pop of fireworks like a puff of breath in Helen's ear.

December 19, 2007: The cruiser's headlights caught the shadows of footprints across the road's new snow, and Helen pulled to the shoulder. The gravel sky looked heavy, the woods flanking Pentland Road lost in a fog of flurries. The footprints disappeared through a gap in the brambles. The girl, Jocey Dempsy, hadn't come home from school, had been gone over a day. Nobody in town had seen or heard from her. Her folks said she often took walks in these woods. Helen retrieved the holster and pistol from the seat beside her. She turned the cruiser's spotlight on the tree line, but could not see through the falling snow. She shut off the engine. The motor ticked in the dark quiet, wet snow piling upon the windshield.

Christmas Eve, 2007: Helen glimpsed her reflection in the door's glass, her battered eye bulged like a stone had risen on her face. Snow curled up the porch steps and over her boots. The door opened. There stood Connie Dempsy wearing a red sweater with snowflakes embroidered in silver thread. She did not say hello, but stepped aside for Helen to pass.

The front hall smelled like popcorn, like cinnamon. A little girl in pajamas, a smiling bear on her belly, hid behind Connie's leg. She was Jocey's baby sister and looked like her. Warm light fell into the hall from the kitchen, and then David was in the light, wiping his hands on an apron. Helen didn't know where to stand. There was no doormat and she did not want to track snow into their house.

"Merry Christmas," she said.

Connie lifted the girl into her arms, would not look at Helen.

"Would you like something to eat?" David asked, still down the hall in the kitchen doorway.

A puddle had formed on the tiles beneath her boots. "I don't have any news," Helen said. They said nothing. Helen held out the pie box, and another package wrapped in green paper with a white ribbon. "Here's one of Freely's pies. And I got something for the girl. It ain't much of anything, but it's something."

They went into the family room, an upright piano in the corner, the tree beside it, tiny colored lights flashing. Helen had removed her boots and was afraid her feet stank; she'd worn the same wool socks five straight days. But all she smelled was popcorn and cinnamon. The family sat on a sofa, the girl in the middle. Helen faced them in a high-back wooden chair, her gun belt awkward against the armrest.

The little girl did not tear the paper like most kids. She picked at the tape, her mother helping, and carefully unfolded the wrapping to reveal a box. Inside was a tiny pink shirt. Across the front were a golden star and the words JUNIOR DEPUTY, KRAFTON POLICE. Connie and David glanced at each other. Light glinted off the silver thread in Connie's sweater. The apron hung down between David's legs. The little girl wrinkled her nose and stared at Helen's face, and Helen was sure she'd ask about her swollen eye.

Helen crossed one socked foot over the other. She looked at Connie. "It ain't much," she said. "I didn't know what to give a child."

December 19, 2007: Helen crossed Pentland Road and pushed through brambles and into the woods. Her flashlight created a tunnel of light, inside of which were the arms of catbrier and low-slung limbs and the occasional shallows of footprints. She pulled her stocking cap to her brow. She felt the immense silence. Helen trudged on, and deeper in, where gray dusk lit the bench above her, she saw tracks of black soil where the snow had been disturbed. Helen climbed, her feet slipping as she scaled the slope, and stopped up on the ridge to examine a scuttle of boot prints.

Slivers of pink broached the flurries in the western sky. She paused, breathing heavily, and stared down over the valley. A black stream cut the mottled white, powdered trees hunched on their hummocks. In one distant corner of the prairie the last of daylight glinted off a tin roof.

Some gentle movement in her periphery made her notice the near trees. Far below, a large white oak still held its autumn leaves, its branches gently waving. Through a gap in its canopy she glimpsed a flash of pale skin. Her breath drew away, and then she was shuffling down the bench and she slipped and fell hard on her back, sliding in the new snow to the base of the slope.

The oak towered above her. She shone her light up into it, over the girl's exposed ribs, her dangling arms, and between her buds of breasts curved a rivulet of dried blood, dripped from where the rope had torn the skin of her neck. Helen turned on her side and retched. Vomit steamed in the dirt. She took clean snow into her mouth and caught her breath. She stood and unsnapped the latch over her pistol, and approached the darkness beneath the boughs.

The girl's toes dangled inches from the ground. She wore only shoes. Clunky black shoes with square heels. Her naked skin glowed white against the dusk. Her mouth hung open and what little light came through the saffron boughs gleamed in her braces. Helen took off her own coat. She tried throwing the jacket up over the girl's shoulders, but it slid off and fell in a lump on the ground.

It was the girl. Jocelyn Dempsy, whom everyone called Jocey. She raced motorbikes on a dirt track by the old mill, played JV basketball as an eighth grader. She loved Moon Pies. Loved cherry cola. She'd come to the grocery and buy them, and Helen would watch her eat alone by the road and return the bottle for a nickel before riding off.

Brisk wind whistled through the limbs. Helen stumbled to sit against the trunk of the oak, her legs stretched out before her, pistol drawn in her lap. Dusk had settled. The prairie was tinted blue, shocks of blue sedge stiffly swaying.

Spring 2008: All day Helen had searched the flooded area, delivered the stranded to higher ground. Now she was alone. The current took the boat and she shone the spotlight across the black water and onto the large house, the flood up to its second-floor sills. She hooked the dock rope around a window box and the prow knocked against the siding. She pressed her forehead to the window's cool glass. The room's red fabric wallpaper had silver stripes that flashed in the spotlight. A twin bed lay diagonally in the middle of the room. A cardboard box made a crater in the mattress, a new-looking ball glove atop the box. Alone on a wall above a dresser hung a poster of three busty women in yellow swimsuits, each suit with two letters that when pressed tightly together spelled YAMAHA.

Helen forced open the window. Careful not to sway the boat, she held her holster and stepped down into the room. It was the first time in hours she'd been out of the boat, and her legs shook. The carpet glistened in the spotlight, a dark line three feet up the wall marking the flood's highest point.

The room had not been disturbed, was kept like a museum; Helen had been in the room that winter, putting on a play of sorts, searching the girl's drawers and beneath her bed and taking notes on what she passed off as evidence—report cards, a menu from the Tahiti Connection restaurant in Turberville, a ticket stub from a motocross event in Bowling Green—she knew would lead nowhere. She wrote it all up in a report for the staties.

The bedroom door was locked from the inside. Helen opened the lock and door, wiped the knob clean, then walked down the hall. Water splashed with each step. The walls were tiled with Dempsy family photos: Jocey, very young, sporting a boy's shag haircut and straddling a small motorbike; the family in matching cream sweaters with David on a hay bale, the baby on his lap, Jocey and Connie each behind one of his shoulders; Jocey's school portrait, a ponytail tied with red ribbon, braces, a blemish on her nose.

At the back of the house, Helen entered the master bedroom. A canopy bed with mahogany posts filled most of the room. Helen gazed out the bedside window at the flooded world, the dark roofs of houses spread like barges on a big river. Everything smelled of soil and fish. So much water, so much washed over, but perhaps when they started anew everything could be better, everything forgiven. Perhaps God would allow the girl to be dredged up by the flood and found, her parents granted their closure, yet the unrighteous cause of her death kept a gracious unknown.

Helen walked to a bureau and searched the drawers, one filled with scarves and nylons, the next with panties neatly folded and separated by color. She moved to the closet and shone her light over the clothes; pants at one end, then blouses, then dresses. Sweaters were on a shelf above the hanging clothes. She pulled the red sweater from the middle of a stack, unfolded it to be sure it was the right one. The silver thread of the embroidered snowflakes twinkled in Helen's spotlight. She held the sweater to her face; it smelled faintly of Connie's perfume. It was an impulse, and Helen could not explain why she needed it other than to say it was something clean and lovely in a world of mud. She hugged the sweater to her throat and lay down on the bed, the mattress soft and pulling her in, her boot heels flat and heavy on the waterlogged carpet.

December 19, 2007: Blue smoke trailed from a pipe in the cabin's tin roof. His footprints had frozen like fossils in the snow, and Helen tracked them down through the prairie. The cabin belonged to Robert Joakes, who came into town once a month for supplies, and sold beaver and coon pelts to a coat maker in Northhill.

A dim light came from the cabin's only window, a small square high up the wall. Helen stood on her numb toes and peered through the window. A lantern on a rough wood table gave a scant circle of light. A figure hunched beside an iron stove. Helen removed a glove and drew her pistol, felt its weight in her hand, adjusted her finger on the trigger. For a good while she watched the dark figure, embers glowing behind the stove grate. Then Joakes moved off into the shadows.

Helen crouched beneath the window. Whittled gray clouds raced in from the north. The wind tore through her. Her hand on the pistol grew terribly cold. A half mile away in the tree, Jocey's body was freezing solid, and Helen felt herself at the center of something enormous and urgent, bigger than her mind could hold, and though terrified, and angry, mainly she felt desperately alone. The urge to flee, to hide, was overwhelming. This is how Jocey felt, Helen thought, and clicked off her pistol's safety.

She eased each step through the crackling snow, past firewood stacked to the roof, on around to the door where a metal bucket gave off the stench of urine. A dog barked inside the door, heavy and loud barking that did not cease.

Christmas Eve, 2007: She followed at a safe distance, as children on inner tubes towed behind a pickup made wide tracks in the road's new snow. More children huddled in the truck's bed, sparklers burning in their mittens and gloves. The truck took the curve of Elm Avenue and the inner tubes swung out, the last in line dropping into the ditch before the whip cracked and yanked it back onto the road. Helen switched on the blue and red lights atop the squad car. The truck did not pull to the shoulder, but merely slowed and stopped, the inner tubes sliding forward, one knocking into the next.

Helen grabbed her flashlight and walked out into the snow, the kids splayed and breathing hard on their tubes.

"We ain't done nothing," said the boy on the last tube, a boy they all called Knight, his chin resting on his gloves.

"Not yet, you ain't," Helen said, and kept the flashlight beam on his face just to get him riled.

"You're piss mean even at Christmas," Knight snapped, and all the other kids laughed.

Helen passed the kids in the truck bed, their sparklers hissing glitter and glistening in their eyes. "You kids cold?"

"No'm," said one boy. "I am," said a girl, and the boy told her to shut up.

Then Helen was at the truck's door, and Willie Sharpton grinned at her, the flaps of his hat down over his ears and a cigarette in the slit between his mustache and beard. Helen put a boot up on the truck's running board and leaned in the window.

"Them kids just grabbed hold of my truck," Willie said. "Don't know whose they are."

"They just lassoed your tailgate?"

"That's about right." Willie blew smoke back into the truck as not to blow it on Helen. He turned and studied her face and closed one of his eyes. "That eye looks like hell."

"Our wedding pictures'll look awful."

It was a play on an old joke, one neither smiled at. Knight yelled for them to come on, that his nuts were freezing. Willie patted Helen's arm and took a drag on the cigarette. He stared ahead where the snow was yet to be tracked by tires.

"Any leads?" he asked.

"No."

Then they were quiet, and Helen stepped down from the truck's runner and looked back at the children. The sparklers had burned out and the bed was dark. Drift snow crawled out of the ditch and side-wound over the road. She shone her flashlight on the line of tubes. The kids had their hoods pulled over their faces.

December 19, 2007: Footsteps and a man's scolding voice came from behind the cabin door. The barking ceased. Flat against the weatherboards, she tried keeping her frozen fingers from gripping the gun too tight. The door unlatched and swung open, its shadow covering her. A large yellow-haired dog ran into the prairie, stopped, raised its head, sniffed at a briar. Joakes stepped out into the snow, shirtless, thick hair covering his shoulders and back. It'd be safer outside, where he couldn't grab a rifle or knife, a chair or a pot. Helen held her breath, her jaw clenched. She lunged out, gun raised, yelled at him to get on the ground.

Joakes flailed around and hit Helen with an elbow, and she slipped to one knee. He paused and glanced over his shoulder, maybe looking for the dog, maybe checking to see if there were others. Helen drove into his legs and he fell to the ground. Forearm under his chin, she pulled Mace from her belt and doused his eyes. He swung his fists. She scrambled out of his reach, then stepped forward and sprayed him again. He covered his face, Mace dripping down his fingers and chin. The dog charged in, sniffing at the man and barking. Helen approached, both pistol and Mace drawn, the dog baring its teeth, yapping, pouncing. She sprayed the dog and it recoiled, pawing its snout, then came at her again, viciously snapping at her legs. She fired the gun. The dog fell in a lump, a hole through its neck, hot blood leaching into the snow. A knee in Joakes's back, Helen pressed the gun to his ear and said she figured to kill him for what he'd done. His eyes were shut tight. He did not move.

Spring 2008: She stared at the canopy's sheer fabric and heard it again: hissing and what sounded like a gunshot. She rose from the Dempsys' bed and stepped to the window. Again came the hissing. In the northern sky the pop unleashed golden sparks that willowed down. On what she knew was Macey Goff's roof stood a silhouette, another whining flare rising from its arm and exploding high above, green sparks shimmering, falling.

Helen held the Christmas sweater to her breast and felt protected, like a child with her blanket. She stuffed it into her jacket, zipped up, and hustled down the damp hall to her boat. She hooked in the oars and began rowing around the house, making for the Goffs'. The current was strong. To keep the boat straight Helen pulled twice on the right oar for each on the left. Across the bay a silver bass boat hitched to a second-floor window thudded against the house. The man on the roof wore jeans tucked into his boots and a sleeveless flannel unbuttoned to show a mural of tattoos across his chest and abdomen. He dropped a Roman candle into the gutter, drew a fresh wand from his boot. He was Danny Martin, a young strip miner who'd been a great ball player, even had offers to play in college, but then he beat up a girl and it all went to hell.

Helen brought in the oars and the boat glided. Blue sparks fell directly above her. A flashlight beam waggled inside the house. Looters. She drew her pistol and switched on the boat's spotlight. Inside the room a large long-haired man in black waders spun around. The spotlight threw his shadow on the back wall, and when he shielded his eyes the shadow took the appearance of a hunchback, then grew larger as he ran to the window. He clanged out into the bass boat, the hull rocking and sliding away from the house.

"Danny!" the man screamed, furiously yanking the motor's cord.

"Stay where you're at!" Helen yelled.

A candle shot whistled low overhead. Helen ducked, trained the spotlight on the roof. Danny toed the gutter, the wand aimed down at her. She spun off the bench and covered her head. A shot hissed into the water beside the boat.

"This is the police!" Helen yelled.

The other boat's outboard turned over and raised an octave speeding away. Then another pop, high overhead, and Helen looked to the sky. Golden sparks rained down. Held in an eddy, her boat slowly turning, red sparks fell, and moments later the sky bled green. Then the candle was done and Danny gazed into the whitecaps thrashing the house. He teetered, raised his arms. He leapt from the roof, his legs scissoring as he hit the water.

December 20, 2007: Robert Joakes sat tied to a chair in the lantern's pitiful light; Helen had torn bedsheets and bound his ankles, wrists, chest, and gagged his mouth so he could not scream.

She'd found Jocey's clothes atop a mound of salted venison in the root cellar, and sat thinking on the cellar steps with the girl's jeans across her lap. Laws on killing, even God's demands, didn't allow for peace. Not always. There'd still be pain; missing that child would break her parents' hearts. But what Helen knew, what she'd seen in those woods, would be too much for them, for everybody.

She made a plan to hide it all, and knew she'd have to be careful. She'd be ruined if Joakes got loose, or if someone found him like this, or if he died too soon. Those in town, and especially those from outside Krafton, might not see grace in her methods: what she'd begun to call in her mind *the Big Peace*.

Spring 2008: Danny emerged far downcurrent, pummeling the churning spate, flopping, thrashing. Helen gave chase, but the current was unpredictable and, afraid she'd brain him with the boat's hull or the outboard's blades, she dared not get close. His body went slack and he was swept toward the ropy tops of willow trees, disappearing into the cage of their branches.

Helen cut the motor and scrambled to the bow. She grabbed several branches as they whisked past and was jerked backward into the stern. The rush of water was amplified in the blackness. She held the ropes and took her feet and balanced herself, and with her free hand switched on the boat's spotlight.

The canopy was a tangle of limbs, the water topped with brown froth and swirling as if over a drain. Danny draped one arm over a thick branch, his cheek against the trunk, his shoulders beneath the water. Helen pulled the boat deeper through the mess. Danny lifted his head, managed to tilt his chin into the tree's crotch. "We was looking for my dog," he said, gasping.

He was a liar, but that didn't matter now. The branch forked into the water and Helen couldn't get to him. She leaned over the branch and reached as far as she could. Danny stared blankly at her hand. His head lolled, his elbow unhooking from the branch, and he held on with just his hand, his body dragging in the current. Helen lunged her entire body onto the branch and grabbed his wrist. She centered her weight and pulled until his elbow was hooked back safely, then dropped her feet down into what she thought would be the boat, but instead was the rush of freezing water.

The boat had drifted from beneath her, the spotlight a trailing beacon as the hull curled into the rope branches, was held briefly, then the limbs parted and fell back into place and the boat was gone. Helen hugged the branch and clutched Danny, the flood whirling darkly around them, the Christmas sweater a lump in the gathers of her jacket.

December 22, 2007: She scanned the frozen prairie, worried someone had seen her sneak through the dawn-tinged woods and into the cabin. Behind her, bound to the chair, Joakes stank of urine and shit. She carefully untied his ankles, then his legs, his waist. Three days in the chair and his legs had atrophied; they buckled as he stood, and he staggered as she walked him to a snowy swale in the river's bend. There she took down his soiled pants and told him to relieve himself. He stood shivering, loins exposed, mouth and upper body still bound, head drooped. He fell to his knees, then onto his side, and began to weep. Helen found him pathetic, disgusting. The sunrise washed full over the eastern hills and burned through shreds of fog in the near woods, and she worried someone would see him. Helen rushed to him, trying to pull up his pants and get him to stand. But he just wept and shook, and Helen could do nothing with him.

She dragged him by his armpits, inch by inch, his pants at his ankles, bare legs wet and red with cold, heels leaving ruts in the snow. She dragged him past the pump frozen over with icicles, and past a stack of vegetable crates covered in snow, in which lived brown chickens that did not move and might be dead. The dog's stiff body lay at the side of the stoop. It would look right that way, Helen figured; a man who kills his dog is a man who's lost all hope.

It took half an hour to get him back in the chair. She removed his pants and covered his lower half with a heavy blanket. She carried the pants to the river, stomped a hole through the ice, and dangled the crotch in the water below. Helen returned and laid the pants over half the stove, turned her nose from the putrid steam. On the other half of the stove, she heated oats in a pot. A square blazon of sunlight flooded the window and covered Joakes's face. His eyes, scorched by the Mace, were a deep watery red, the skin not covered by beard the color of tin.

Helen unbound his mouth and pushed oatmeal on a wooden spoon between his lips. He took the oats into his cheeks and she pushed in another spoonful. He stared through her, his red eyes narrowed in the sunlight, and for a moment she remembered what he'd done, and stood frozen before him.

He spat the oats into her face. He licked his lips. "I'm a Christian man," he said, hoarsely, oats in the beard beneath his mouth. "I'm forgiven."

Christmas Day, 2007: Freely sat in a lounger by the fire, a blanket over his lap, his eyelids batting, then closing. Helen sat on the hearthstone ledge, the fire hot on her back. She'd not worn her uniform for the first time in a long while, and found her old jeans to be loose in a way she'd greatly missed. On the floor by the tree a circle of children played a game where they rolled dice and moved tiny farm animals around a board. The adults sat around a long table, drinking hazelnut coffee and discussing a new foundry opening in Jasper. Helen's feet prickled with pain and she worried they were frostbitten. Her swollen eye gave a headache aspirin could not help.

The front bell rang. Freely's wife, Marilyn, walked to the foyer, wiping her hands on the back of her dress. She opened the door and in rushed the cold and the children sat upright to see who was there. Pastor Hamby, a bear of a man in a black overcoat, filled the door-way. Marilyn stepped aside to let him in, but he stayed where he was. He leaned down and talked quietly to Marilyn and glanced into the house at the same time. Then Marilyn turned and they both looked at Helen, and Pastor Hamby waved her over with a gloved hand.

Helen stepped gingerly out on the porch and closed the door be-hind her. Four men in parkas, the First Baptist deacons, stood at dif-ferent levels on the steps, colored lights in the spruce reflecting on tracks of ice on the porch. Helen did not have her coat, and hugged herself with one arm and sipped her coffee.

Pastor Hamby's cheeks were flushed, his thin lips drawn tightly over his teeth. "We were delivering care baskets out in the knobs like we always do," he said, and looked back at the deacons.

They'd found Joakes's body, this Helen knew by their faces. She tried to still her own face, her heart, to quiet the guilty part of her that wanted to confess and be forgiven.

Frank Barker, a squat man in glasses, stepped a boot on the porch and leaned over his leg. "The holidays is hard on some," he said. "It ain't joy and cranberries for everyone. For some it's only lonesome pain."

Spring 2008: Willow limbs hung limply in the brightening morn, the current's froth filling with light and bending prisms where black branches emerged. All night Helen had listened in darkness to the flood's drone, and in a waking dream she'd seen the girl's body float up from the quarry depths, drift and drift in the murky current to be caught in the high branches of one of the town's ancient oaks, and as the water receded, her neck wedged in a crook, there the girl dangled above Old Saints Road for all to see.

Now Helen sat high in the willow and tore away limbs until she could see out over the water. A single ridge humped out in the east. Her boat was nowhere to be seen. Danny was in a sort of sleep. She'd given him Connie Dempsy's Christmas sweater, and handcuffed his wrists to a branch overhead so he would not fall. His head hung in the hammock of his arms, the sweater too small and the sleeves far up his wrists.

To the north, sunlight winked off the hull of a bass boat. Helen screamed and screamed, but with the rushing water she knew she would not be heard. She drew her pistol and fired into the gap of sky. She fired twice more before the boat veered their way, then fired again to keep the boat on track.

Once it was close enough, she began to holler. She glanced below at Danny, who picked up his head and stared up at her, the sweater stretched tight across his chest, the silver snowflakes twinkling. He too began to scream, and Helen could see the boat was steered by the long-haired looter from the night before. He cut the motor, the hull piled high with bodies of dogs.

The prow parted the canopy and Helen stared down between her legs, the long-haired man watching her as he passed below. Danny called out to his friend, and the boat bumped against the trunk. The long-haired man held the tree with one hand, and with the other lifted a shotgun to his shoulder and aimed it at Helen.

"No, Ray," Danny said. "She's all right." Danny was staring up at her, and asked, "You all right, ain't you?"

Helen nodded, held her hands out where he could see them.

"She's all right, Ray," Danny said again, and the man in the boat let the gun fall to his side.

Helen uncuffed Danny and they both climbed carefully into the boat, and had to sit on the same tiny bench to avoid the dogs. Dogs filled the hull; a collie atop a German shepherd, and several hunting dogs, blueticks and grays. Stacked in an orderly way, heads at one end, tails the other, stacked like firewood. The boat drifted from beneath the tree, willow branches washing over them and then the sun was warm. Thin clouds feathered out above. Ray stuffed his lip with chaw and stared Helen down. "Found a body," he said, then turned away and wrapped the cord around the outboard flywheel.

Christmas Eve, 2007: Robert Joakes quietly sobbed, lips smacking as if from thirst, and asked to smoke just one cigarette. Helen considered it a moment, then untied his right arm. She carried the lantern to the cupboard and pushed aside a jar of pickled eggs, and there was the thin wooden box. The smell of tobacco came out strong. She kept the lid open, hoping the smell would overtake the odors of Joakes himself. She even held it beneath Joakes's nose. He shut his eyes and seemed to take solemn pleasure from the scent. Then he opened his lids and his red eyes drew onto her.

He snatched the lantern like trap jaws sprung, and Helen was struck in the face and fell hard to the floor. The lantern light was gone. Moonlight through the tiny window lit a back wall where skinning tools hung on metal pegs. Freezing pain ripped through Helen's eye, her skull. Chair legs thumped as Joakes fumbled with his free hand to untie his bindings. Her face swelled quickly; within seconds the eye was closed to sight. Dizzily, Helen took her feet and drew her pistol. She stayed still until she found the pale skin of his bald spot in the moonlight. Helen struck and Joakes shrieked. With all her weight she struck him once more. Joakes's head bobbed violently, and he made no sound.

Helen staggered into the yard, clutching her gun, and broke an icicle off the pump's handle. She lay back in the snow, dim stars turning in fractured tracks, the frozen ground beneath her seeming to turn, and though she meant to hold the ice to her eye, she brought up the pistol and it was cold and soothed her just the same.

December 20, 2007: Parked on the quarry's service road, the cruiser growing cold with the motor off, Helen sipped peppermint schnapps and considered the world made of her design. My religion is keeping peace, she thought. It hadn't begun that way, was nothing she'd planned, but now she saw that's how it was. I just ran a grocery, she thought. I don't want this. I ain't the one to make the world right. She swallowed more schnapps, then capped the bottle and put it away in the glove box.

Helen stepped out onto the road and popped the trunk. The air had warmed, the boreal wind stilled. Like ashes from a furnace, thick and gentle snow began to fall. She'd taken the clothes from Joakes's root cellar, washed them in the river, dressed the girl. She'd wrapped the girl in a green canvas tarp. Helen struggled lifting the body from the trunk. But she tugged and heaved the torso out over the fender and the rest followed. Helen had needed a sled, and without knowing its use Freely sold her one at half price, and now she turned the green canvas parcel onto the sled, a sheet of red plastic tethered with rope.

She hauled Jocelyn Dempsy on the sled, the girl's weight breaking the undercrust of old snow, dredging new snow in wet mounds about her head and shoulders. Helen pressed onward, eyes closed to the cold, legs plodding into drifts.

At the quarry's rim she paused to unfasten the tarp. She did not look at the girl. She moved behind the sled and shoved it all over. From her knees she watched the sled and tarp flutter, and the body turn and break through the film of ice with barely a sound.

Flakes fused to flakes and piled on her thighs and gloves. The quarry would soon be thick with ice, and what was below would be held for a time. In spring the body would ascend through the gray slush and be found. The town told stories of children who'd fallen to their deaths in this quarry. Teenagers were drawn to its danger. They would all believe Jocey had just drowned, and it would be over. Helen gazed down into the quarry. This is how I'll be, she thought. I'll be this icy hole, this season, this falling snow. I'll just freeze myself over.

Spring 2008: In the flume between hillocks the floodwaters converged, dammed by logs and mud, a kitchen chair, a section of roof, a child's plastic slide, refuse thick and high and brown water sluicing through random gaps. A frenzy of gulls hovered, filling the sky, the refuse wall alive with white birds. Ray ran the boat onto the grassy hillside. He hopped out and stomped the anchor into the soft earth. Helen climbed cautiously over the mound of dogs, a glove to her nose, Danny close behind. Scum water churned at the dam's base. The torrent on the other side, the swollen Big Squirrel River, charged madly east. Helen feverishly scanned the refuse. The tan face of a mare, what looked like a carousel pony, stuck out from beneath what might be a green canvas tarp. Helen's hands trembled; she'd lost control of her hands. She stuffed them in her pockets, and clenched them into fists thinking of Jocey's school portrait on the evening news, remembering Freely, only weeks ago, taking down the same picture from his diner window.

They climbed the hill where rail tracks split the ridge, and stood on the wooden ties. Down by the river lay swine, a black-faced sheep, more dogs. Helen thought of Haley Winters's cattle. Where'd all those cattle gone?

Ray pointed at an outcropping of rock. A body lay on a slab of limestone, fully clothed, feet spread apart. A gull roosted on the body's shoulder, and Helen could not see the face. "I seen that boy some in the Old Fox," Ray said. "Don't know his name. Never said so much as hey to me."

Helen rushed down the hillside, her momentum carrying her in a reckless sort of run. Wind blew the long grass flat. She followed the grass down with her eyes and tripped and slid hard on her side. The gull on the body raised its wings, flapped twice, and glided down-shore. It wasn't Jocey. It was Keller Lankford, a hay and bean farmer who lived south of town, nearly three miles from the river. His face was the blue of his overalls, his blackened fingers clawed into a fence slat clutched to his chest.

Helen was relieved, horrified. Her body shook, then Danny was over her pleading, *Don't do that, oh come on now,* and pulled her into his arms. Helen shoved him away. She tried taking her feet, only to crumble. Her ankle was badly hurt. She wiped sweat from her eyes and face, noticed small cuts had brought blood to her palms. "Take off that sweater!" Helen screamed at Danny, blood streaked across her cheeks. "Throw it in the river. It ain't yours to be wearing."

Ray was down breaking twigs and tossing them into the current, water climbing the legs of his waders. "Get rid of them dogs!" she shrieked at Ray. "Nobody wants to see them dogs. Just let 'em be gone. You hear what I say?" Ray snapped a twig and brought it to his mouth. He waved up with his middle finger. Danny ran past Ray, thigh deep into the raging flood, and he tore the red sweater off over his head, balled it up, and hurled it into a rush of gulls.

Christmas morning, 2007: Helen wore a rain poncho over her coat, wore yellow rubber gloves. She held the lantern to Robert Joakes's swollen face. Faint plumes of breath trickled from his lips. With a wooden spoon she pried open his mouth, then pushed the spoon and his head tipped backward. She considered, as she had many times before, asking him *why*. But what could he possibly say? What insight could possibly be gleaned? Instead, she inserted the barrel of a shotgun into his mouth. He made noises, not words, gagging on the metal. She set the lantern on the stove, raised her poncho's hood, turned away her face, and squeezed her gloved thumb over the trigger.

The explosion in the small room rattled the cupboards. A ringing pulsed in Helen's ears. Joakes had toppled in his chair and lay in the dark of the floor. She worked fast, looking only when she had to, untying his legs and thighs, his hands and chest, blood pooling blackly over the uneven planks. She worried momentarily as to which hand was his shooting hand, then chose his right, and worked his thumb onto the trigger.

She piled the bindings into a garbage bag, along with the blood-splattered poncho and rubber gloves. She left the lantern burning on the table, hurried outside, careful with her footprints, stepping sideways into drifts so the snow would collapse, then on the exposed rocks behind his house, up the hill, breaking the ice and splashing through a tiny brook, then down the bluff to the frozen stream, where she paused atop a granite boulder.

The moon was in its descent, the stars fading. She'd wait for dawn, for pale light to arise and cover her. She thought of Freely's grandchildren tearing pretty paper from gifts, singing "Away in a Manger" in church. She thought of families gathered around tables thick with holly. In her mind, she tasted honey-glazed ham, scalloped potatoes, macaroons.

But she could not wait for dawn. Her feet were wet, the night bitterly cold. She clutched her collar and limped along the stony banks, and stepping up to enter the prairie she slipped and fell onto the garbage bag of rags and slid until she was out on the frozen stream. The ice popped, but held. Thistles of pain stabbed her toes. She lay on the brittle black ice and could hear water flowing beneath her.

Spring 2008: The men had come down the hill from the shelter and now gathered around the boat. They were solemn, unshaven, shirts rumpled, the pits of Pastor Hamby's white shirt stained with sweat. The farmer's body lay in the hull where once had been dogs, Helen's jacket shrouding his face. The sun was high, the air damp. A new wall of thunderheads and the fur of rain bulged forth in the west.

"You'll tell the others?" Helen said.

Pastor Hamby nodded. "What can we do for *you*?"

"I need rest," Helen said, wilting, and almost began to cry from tiredness. "Let me rest awhile."

Suddenly came the wind, full and strong, and Helen's coat blew off Keller Lankford and tumbled onto the hillside, exposing his blue bloated face. Helen lunged after her coat. Her ankle gave and she caught herself as she fell. A deacon, Jerry Timlinson, clambered into the boat and covered the dead man's face with his own jacket, then squinted up at the approach of weather.

Spatterings of rain fell sideways in wind and sunshine. Pastor Hamby and Frank Barker lifted Helen, each with a hand beneath her thigh and another at her back. Slate clouds rowed forward over the sun, its light dappling the hill and then the sunshower was a storm.

The men entered the lightless hall, shirts transparent with rain, Helen riding their arms. "Put me down," she said, clutching their shirtsleeves. Pale faces emerged from the darkness, Walt Freely and Marilyn, Connie and David Dempsy, the little girl held to his shoulder, everyone she knew, grimly nodding, touching her pant legs, stroking her wrists, some speaking her name with quiet reverence. "Let me down," she repeated, but they did not, and Helen began to cry. Rain drummed the masonry. Light from the storm laid a greenish glow in the hall. She could not stop herself from crying. They huddled around Helen, silent in the gloam, then the pastor raised his pulpit voice and called for them all to just clear out and leave her be.

FURLOUGH

Plywood covered where once had been glass, and Jorgen strained his eyes to find her in the dark bar. Yesterday, a deer charged its reflection and crashed through the Old Fox's front window. Bucks acted crazy during their rut. Things like that happened. But Jorgen was weary of hearing about it, and didn't bother saying hello to Mildred, who sat scratching a lottery ticket behind her bar, or to Pervis Hagen and Ed McDonaghey, who were playing their nightly game of cribbage, as he made his way back to Mary Ellen Landers.

Mary Ellen leaned against the busted jukebox, sipping soda through a straw. She wore a red sequined top, had curled her hair. "What you doing here?" she asked.

"Tad sent me," he said.

"He ain't coming?"

"He'll be where I'm taking you."

She smiled. "What's all this?"

"Can't say."

"A surprise?"

Jorgen shrugged, then called over to Mildred that he needed a couple shots of whiskey. She waved a hand and told him to get it himself. Jorgen never sat down. He led Mary Ellen to the bar and poured the drinks and together they downed the shots.

"You got a coat?" he asked her.

"I need a coat?"

"You can have mine," Jorgen said. "It ain't that far to walk."

Jorgen helped her on with his jacket. He was a small man and it fit her well. His hands lingered on her shoulders. He could smell her perfume, and pulled her hair out from the collar. She smiled as he zipped the coat high to her neck.

"You going to get cold?" she asked.

"I don't get cold."

The night hung a damp chill. Jorgen stuffed his hands in his pockets, nodded for Mary Ellen to follow. They passed the vacant savings and loan, then the First Baptist Church, set back off the road, its steeple glowing white in the darkness. They talked awhile about the freight yard, where Jorgen used to work and Mary Ellen still did, where since he'd been home on furlough, and had nowhere else to go, Jorgen spent his afternoons watching Tad and the boys unload the trains.

Hickory trees rustled overhead. Wet leaves papered the road. Jorgen had once been at the center of things, with everyone else, but then he went to serve overseas, in that desert land, and though he'd been back awhile he felt as gone here as he had over there.

They passed the Langstroms' big Victorian, warm light gathered in its windows. Jorgen watched old lady Langstrom in a nightgown and curlers pull the shade on an upper window, and the light went dark inside.

"What's my surprise?" Mary Ellen asked. "I know you know something about it."

"I don't," he said.

"You know where we're going."

"Ain't going to spoil it."

"Come on, Genie," she begged.

Jorgen kept walking.

"Is it big?" she asked. "At least tell me that."

"Ain't for me to say."

"You know what?" she asked.

"What?"

"I don't like calling you Genie," she said. "I know the boys do, but it don't fit you right. I'm going to call you Jorgen."

Jorgen shrugged. "It's my name."

"I like it," she said, and took his arm. "Jorgen," she said, trying it out. "Jorgen, can I ask you something?"

"I guess."

"You think Tad'll ever marry me?"

The last house in the row sat dark. Three trucks parked bumper to bumper in its gravel drive. Jorgen glanced at Mary Ellen's hand on his arm, her slender fingers, nails painted white at the tips. "That what you want?"

"I think so," she said. "Don't tell him I asked."

Jorgen nodded. A figure stood beneath a willow tree at the corner of the house. Jorgen watched the figure slide out of the curtain of branches, scramble through the house's shadows, then dash into the field they were approaching.

Mary Ellen bubbled, tugged at his wrist. "Hey, Jorgen?"

"Yeah?"

"How long till you got to go back?"

"Back?"

"Over there?"

"Oh," he said. "Not long."

"You know," she said. "I got a cousin I should set you up with.

Crystal's only seventeen, but she's grown for her age, and so smart and pretty. I think you'd all do good together. Boy, she's a wild one." They walked beyond the row of houses and the road became a corridor between fields of corn. Mary Ellen told a story about her cousin sneaking off to the city, where at fifteen she lied about her age and got a job in a casino. "Served a senator once," Mary Ellen said. "Had a Pabst Blue Ribbon." She laughed. "We thought she was at choir practice, if you can believe that. Boy, my uncle tore into her. But when she told him how much she made, he said he knew where she'd work once she got old enough."

The wind blew in the corn and Mary Ellen clung to his arm. "She sounds all right," Jorgen said.

"My uncle was only kidding, though. He wouldn't really want her working there. He's a religious man."

"Oh."

"I used to be more religious than I am now," Mary Ellen said. "I don't know. All that talk on how to live."

Jorgen nodded.

"You're kind of quiet tonight."

"I guess."

"That's what I like about you," Mary Ellen said. "Was just telling Tad about how you sit on that bench by the office, in all that noise, trains going every which way, and it's like you're out fishing on a pond or something. Whenever things're getting tight on me, I just look out at you, you know."

Jorgen watched the corn. A few rows in, stalks were bending more than what the wind could do. "I wasn't always this way."

"Well, it's a good way to be."

The corn wavered, the stiff leaves rustling, sounding like rain on tin. Jorgen began to shiver. He reached his arm around Mary Ellen and pulled her so they had to walk slower.

"I ain't getting cute," he said. "I'm cold is all."

"Thought you said you didn't get cold?"

"Never had before."

"You want your jacket back?" she said. "Maybe we can take turns? A minute for you, a minute for me?"

"I'm all right."

Mary Ellen threw an arm around his waist and they walked easy. The air smelled of woodsmoke. He tried not to look at the corn, but it wouldn't stop shifting in his periphery. Finally, he peered into the rows. "They's dogs that run these fields," he said. "Sometimes the stalks move and you think someone's out there, but it's just the dogs."

Mary Ellen looked into the corn, too. "You trying to spook me?"

"Sometimes, when they cut the crop they find dogs, dead or froze up in a rut or something."

"That's awful."

He shrugged.

"Jorgen," she said. "I ever tell you about my big dream?"

Up ahead, the road came to a T. An abandoned farmhouse sat on a wooded hill above the road, the moonlight edging its chimney and tattered roof. Beside the house, the tops of trees swirled in the wind. "Marrying Tad?"

She smacked his shoulder. "Not that," she said. "No, I want to go to school to work in an animal hospital. That's what my mama does." She chuckled. "We got eleven dogs, two snakes, and a potbellied pig, all what live in the house."

"Must stink."

"You get used to it after a while," she said. "I miss it when I'm gone, if you can believe that."

"I got a bird," he said.

"A bird?"

"A little parakeet."

"What's she called?"

Jorgen felt uneasy. "Don't know," he said. "Never called it nothing." Mary Ellen smacked his shoulder again, laughed like he'd told a joke. He watched her mouth, the white of her teeth, the gap in the front. "Tried to set it free today, but it wouldn't go."

"What you want to set it free for?"

"Just seemed right," Jorgen said. "With me leaving and all. Anyway, it wouldn't go."

"Bet you treat it well."

"It don't say one way or the other."

"It didn't fly off," she said. "That's how it says."

"I guess."

"You might be too nice for my cousin," Mary Ellen said. "She'd eat you alive."

"I ain't that nice."

At the T in the road, Jorgen pointed to the right and they turned onto Old Saints Highway. He walked and watched the farmhouse. A flashlight blinked on and off behind a second-floor window. The right side of the road was a high wall of corn, the left was harvested hills. On a far knob in the middle of the bare field, a tiny light winked back.

"You're shivering like a kitten," Mary Ellen said, and stopped in the road and took off the jacket. "Here, take this awhile."

Jorgen pushed it away. "I'm all right."

"Take it," she said.

"No."

Mary Ellen defiantly stepped forward and wrapped the jacket around Jorgen and held the collar at his throat. "You wear it till I count to sixty," she said, and began to count.

Jorgen breathed in her perfume. She grinned, mouthing the numbers. He could see how it happens. He wanted to throw his arms around her. Kiss her mouth. At the count of twenty, a knot of guilt welled high inside his chest, and he had to look away. Dark things moved out in the field. "There's them dogs," he said, quietly. Mary Ellen glanced over her shoulder, then looked back at him, nodding her head from side to side, whispering *thirty-two, thirty-three.*

"Mary Ellen," he said. "You know that boy what fills the soda machines? Tim Eddy Jenkins?"

Mary Ellen's head stilled. Her mouth stopped counting. "Why's he coming up?"

Jorgen shrugged.

She let loose of his collar. "He's always kind to me," she said, but her eyes turned the shape someone else's eyes might only take when crying. Her body brushed against his as she ran a finger along the skin above his ear. "You ought to let your hair grow out. The army's got you looking like a little boy." She gently slid the jacket off Jorgen's shoulder. "That's sixty."

"I just don't like the way he sings and all," he said. "Coming in with that old squeeze box, putting on a big show for you. Somebody might think something of it."

Mary Ellen put on the jacket. "You're just jealous he *can* sing," she said, and began to walk ahead of him.

Jorgen lagged behind. "I can sing."

"Then sing something," she said curtly, back over her shoulder.

The wind blew and Jorgen rubbed his arms. "I don't sing to people," he said. "I only ever sang to my bird."

"Right," she said. "Well, if I hop around and flap my arms, will you sing to me?"

He shook his head.

"All talk," she said. "Just like Tad and all them others."

Jorgen stopped walking. "I ain't like them."

Then Mary Ellen stopped, too, and reached back and snatched his hand the way a big sister might that of her baby brother. They walked holding hands, past a knob littered with shorn stalks. The land dropped away from the road. Deep in the swale stood a lone sycamore. Beneath it sat the silhouette of a four-wheeler. If Jorgen hadn't known to look for it, he wouldn't have seen it out there in the shadows. The corn to the south rattled in the wind, and he could barely hear the motor as the ATV, small and black as a beetle, drove up and over a ridge. Mary Ellen's hand was warm in his. Across the field and atop the hill sat the aluminum garage, windowless, dark.

They'd come too far, were too close now to turn back. Just ahead lay the gravel drive leading up to the garage. Jorgen sensed the others up there, hiding, watching. It was wrong, what they were doing, and Jorgen felt sick, his neck stiff, his throat raw. "I write songs, you know?"

"Songs?" she said, with a wry smile. "For your bird?"

"Ain't really songs, I guess. Just things I write."

"What kind of things?"

"Just things on my mind."

"Your mind?" She chuckled. "Well, I'd surely like to see that."

"Ain't never showed nobody."

"Not even your bird?" She squeezed his hand.

"No," he said. "I mean, ain't nobody ever know it came from me. I sent one in the mail, but it ain't got my name on it."

"You *mailed* it?"

"Didn't put my name on it, though."

"What?" Mary Ellen asked. "Why?"

"Why what?"

"What're you talking about?"

"Things I write."

"No," she said. "I mean, why not put your name on it?"

He pulled his hand from hers, was afraid she'd feel him tremble. "Don't know." He stuffed his hands in his pockets. "Guess so it's just about what it says, and not who sent it."

"What?" she said. "Aw, you're kidding me."

"Know what I wrote?"

"What?"

"It said, I think you ought to know that I'm fucking your girl."

She chuckled once, glanced away. "Lord, you got a screw loose."

He shrugged.

"Still," she said. "It's kind of funny. Can you imagine?"

Jorgen studied her face in the moonlight, her wilted lips, her downcast eyes. In his mind, he saw that sheer curtain, the blue flickering light from a television. "One night," he said, "I was walking these old roads, you know, and I seen something through a window I wasn't supposed to, and that got me thinking how you could hurt someone more without guns or bombs or none of that shit."

She looked off at the low moon. "You're crazy."

He watched his own boots, the cracked pavement passing. "Anyway," he said, "I only sent one letter."

"Yeah," she said, and kicked a hunk of asphalt. "To who, the Easter Bunny?"

Jorgen could feel himself coming untethered, like he often had over there, where kids slept in the dust and nothing got buried and everything felt like it wasn't quite real. He grabbed Mary Ellen's hand and pulled it to his lips, pressed the back of her hand to his cheek. He felt her pull away, or maybe it was him. She said his name, and then he was crying, and he let go of her hand and ran across the road and jumped down into the ditch. She followed, and then they were in the field, treading over the nubs of corn.

"Hey, big dummy," she called. "Where you going?"

He shook his head.

"Come on, Genie." She hooked her arm around his elbow and turned him back toward the road.

"I'm trying to tell you something," he said, but he couldn't think how to explain himself. His mind was a mess. All he could see were figures on a couch, a dead deer on a barroom floor.

"Will you take care of my bird?" he finally said.

"That what this is all about?"

"Tad and them others ain't worth a shit."

"All right," she said. "Sure."

He nodded. "Don't know who else to ask."

"Poor thing."

Jorgen swallowed hard, took a breath. "I'm just tired is all."

She grinned. "I was talking about the bird."

He was exhausted, was sure if he fell he'd never get back up again. "Don't sleep much no more. I just walk around, you know," he said. "All night I just walk around."

She rubbed his arm. "I appreciate you taking me out here."

He tried to focus. "The cold don't bother me."

"We going to the garage?"

Jorgen nodded.

"So much for romance," Mary Ellen said, and laughed a sigh. Then she tugged his hand, stopped them both. "You all right?"

He forced a smile, shrugged.

She smirked, too. "I'll call my mama. Get you some pills that'd put a mule to sleep."

Jorgen's smile faded. They climbed the hill in silence. Jorgen thought about stopping, but he took one step and then the next. Low clouds drifted overhead. In a gap of open sky, tiny red lights from an airplane blinked, then slid behind the clouds. Jorgen watched the lights appear again, for but a moment, before they were gone.

They stood in the gravel drive in front of the garage. The ATV sat in the tall grass beside the door. Dogs lay atop a rusted-out car. A German shepherd, face matted over with mud, hobbled out of the grass with one gimpy leg.

"Tad said to knock three times," Jorgen told Mary Ellen.

She hurried toward the garage. Jorgen trailed her, the old dog at his heels. He'd just wanted to be part of something. His whole life, that's all he'd ever wanted. That's why he'd enlisted, had gone overseas.

More dogs trotted around the building, bounding about Jorgen, sniffing low at the garage. Mary Ellen stopped at the door. She took off his jacket and tried to hand it to him.

"I don't want it," he said. He helped her back on with the jacket, zipped it up. He peered into her eyes, hoping a kind of understanding had passed between them.

She grinned, kissed his cheek.

Then he looked off at the fields. He heard the three rattling knocks on the aluminum door. The dogs barked. The door clacked as it raised, and light burst over them as the gang inside hollered like a surprise party.

The buck deer was strung up with chains from the rafters, was draped in a red gown. They'd painted its hooves red and tied a bouquet to one, stapled a blond wig and a big white hat to its skull. Beside it sat Tim Eddy Jenkins, bound to a chair with silver tape. His nostrils trailed blood, the old squeeze box between his hands. Tad, in a powder-blue suit, hair slicked back, struck Tim Eddy's legs with a switch and Tim Eddy pulled apart the bellows and sound, not quite music, screeched out. The boys whooped. Tad took the buck by the forelegs and pretended to dance.

Mary Ellen backed into Jorgen. She stared as if to recognize him. Jorgen shoved her into the road, and she was enough of a local to know to run. Dogs ran along with her, barking, and the boys piled out howling as they gave chase down the hill. Tad ran the hill, too, far behind the others.

Mary Ellen didn't stay on the road. Jorgen watched her descend the berm and break headlong into the corn. The boys followed her in.

Their shouts fell muffled. Halfway down, Tad sat on the gravel road, then lay back and covered his face with an arm.

Jorgen shuffled slowly down, his hands in his pockets. He stood beside Tad, who sat upright and wiped tears with his sleeve. "I just loved her so much," he said. Jorgen nodded, watched the flats far below. A couple of boys came out of the rows, Mary Ellen nowhere to be seen. Tad smacked Jorgen's leg. "Hey," he said, and reached up a hand. "It's good to have ol' Genie back."

Jorgen stared at the hand. He pulled his hands from his pockets, hugged himself against the cold. The others were emerging from the corn and climbing the ditch bank, shouting, laughing. Jorgen walked down. He passed through them all. One of them asked where he was going, but he didn't answer. He crossed the highway and sidestepped down the ditch and pushed into the corn.

Jorgen wandered a long while, pressing deeper into the field, corn leaves raking his neck and face, his boots heavy with mud. Then he stopped. The wind had stilled, the world hushed.

Jorgen stomped a mat of stalks on which to lie. Moonlight seeped over him. He gazed into the muzzy stars, thought of the freight yard, of watching the boys load lumber and pallets of feed and steel forms from the Leighton foundry.

Over in the war, to lull himself to sleep, he'd play in his mind the trains coming and going. Jorgen wondered if once he got back over there he'd have the same patrol. He recalled a spot on his loop, a crater burned into a hillside, where each night he'd sit and glass the valley of stone, the land as bright as milk in the moonlight, until the others caught up and he'd have to return to the road.

FORT APACHE

The electric sign for the Krafton Bowl and Lounge was a vibrant white square atop a tall post. Set back from the road, the lounge's roof and all but one wall had collapsed. Smoldering lumber jutted from charred brick. Bowling lanes lay exposed to the night, and in the lane oil lapped tiny spectral flames like a riot of hummingbirds. Firemen shoveled dirt over the lanes. Others held blankets at the building's corners. A tuft of sparks rose from a joist and drifted down onto the dry prairie, where a man smothered it beneath a stretch of wool.

Walt trailed his brother Lonnie and little nephew, Calvin. His eyes stung. His nostrils burned. Today was his birthday, and he fanned away smoke with the gray fedora he'd bought hoping to look a bit like Bogie or Cagney, even Ladd, any of the picture-show toughies. Smoke hazed the road. Under the sign's electric glow, a bare-chested man leaned against the post, breathing hard into a paper sack.

"Anyone harmed?" Lonnie called to the man.

The fireman crumpled the sack, stared down at Calvin. Lonnie let the boy smoke to keep him quiet and a cigarette dangled from his lips. "Say," the man said, "you got more of that tobacco?"

Lonnie pulled a cigarette from his pocket. The fireman took it in his blackened fingers, stooped to light it off the end of Calvin's. Smoke seeped from his lips as he rose. His eyes narrowed on the sky. High overhead tumbled a wing of burning ash. The fireman backed under it, turned on his heels, raced across the road.

"Hey," Lonnie shouted, "how'd it start?"

"Small fires make big fires," the fireman called back, wading into the prairie, tripping circles beneath the drifting embers, staggering through the high grabbing grass.

In the sign's pale light, Walt studied his brother's eyes, bright and blue and tracking the ash's flight. Then they drew onto Walt.

"Small fires make big fires," Lonnie said, with lilting reverence. "I surely hope so."

They descended the hill into town. Sharpton's Hardware was dark, with red, white, and blue streamers draping its windows. Mounds of produce lay in front of the general store, and amid them a goat asleep with its beard between its hooves. Up the road stood the tall brownstone that housed the picture show. Over the sidewalk, over the golden stars stenciled onto the concrete, hung the marquee.

DOUBLE FEATURE:

FAR FRONTIER

&

FORT APACHE

Lonnie cut into the side alley. Walt followed, Calvin clutching his hand. They passed rancid Dumpsters and crates shimmering white with sleeping pigeons. The back side of the building opened onto listless prairie, the sedge undotted but for an old telegraph depot gone to ruin.

They stopped at a metal door, and Lonnie yanked it open. A frail boy in a red usher's jacket and bow tie stood guard inside— Lester Muncie, a former schoolmate who'd been two grades ahead of Walt. Lester grabbed for the door, but in one fluid movement Lonnie shoved Lester and wedged a hip in the jamb.

Lester didn't fight. He turned back into the flickering darkness, his eyes on the screen, and pretended not to see them hurrying past.

The first movie was ending. Orchestra horns blared as Roy Rogers rode Trigger through a shadow-cut arroyo. Walt climbed the stairs into the balcony and the music faded and the houselights bloomed. Up in the top row, Frances, Lonnie's girl and Calvin's mother, sat beside her sister Georgette. Hep James, Lonnie's best friend, sat two rows down. Lonnie settled into the aisle seat beside Frances, and Calvin hopped onto his mother's lap.

"Hey, Walt," Frances said. "That's a swell hat you got."

"Ain't you the movie star," Georgette said.

Walt sat beside Hep, who'd have been handsome if not for a scar across his left eye and cheek. Just after Hep returned from the war, some boy slashed him with a switchblade in an alley behind a bar up in the city. Hep had lived for a time in the city, but after that he came home.

"Roy surely got beat to hell and back in that one," Hep said, slumped in his seat.

"And not a scratch on him," Walt joked.

Hep looked perturbed. "Where'd you get that dumb hat?"

"It's a gift," Walt said, embarrassed. "Haley wants me to wear it on the berry wagon. Says folks'll buy better if I look more sophisticated."

Hep sneered. "Haley want doilies in the shit house, too?"

Lonnie called down, "Bowling alley's got burned up."

Hep snapped upright, turned to Lonnie. "Fire get anyone?"

"Nah." Lonnie sounded disappointed.

Hep slid down again and propped his boots on the seat in front of him. "Well," he said, "life ain't a goddamn movie."

In the booth behind them, the projectionist loaded a reel. Calvin rolled himself along the red velvet covering the walls. Frances looked grave whispering in Lonnie's ear. Georgette came and sat beside Walt, smiling with soda-wet lips, a dab of licorice stuck in her teeth.

"Having a fun birthday?" she asked.

"What's it to you?"

"I can help you have fun is what."

Hep elbowed Walt, loudly sniffing.

Walt didn't know what Hep meant by this, though he knew it was vulgar. To avoid Georgette's gaze, he leaned out over his knees. The balcony was five rows, and beyond was the open expanse of the theater. Directly below the screen, town kids congregated around a marble wishing well. Marilyn Garfield, the girl Walt wanted to love, was down there. She wore a green skirt and stood with one leg straight, like a ballerina. That spring, she'd told him he looked like Montgomery Clift and he decided she was the one.

But Walt had never spoken to Marilyn beyond selling her berries. He was seventeen, slight for his age. By his whiskerless cheeks, one might think him younger. Moreover, the same childish fear he once had of going into their dark stables, or being alone in his bed at night, had taken hold of Walt. He glanced back at Lonnie, who'd been in the war, and who now sat listening to Frances prattle on, and wondered if his brother had for even a single moment been as afraid as he was at all times.

———

The lights dimmed and everyone took their seats. The projector beam flowed above Walt's fedora. Up on screen, an aging soldier rode in a stagecoach beside a teenage Shirley Temple. Her eyes were those of the little girl Walt had seen in so many films. But now she was a woman named Philadelphia, and she strolled a desert fort in a petticoated dress. She asked another woman if she'd help fix up her father's place.

Without a conscious moment of sliding, Walt was inside the screen, there on that dusty road behind the battlements, the sun sweltering above and everything of this world gone—the red fabric walls, the stuttering projector, Hep and Georgette, and the whole shitty town.

"How's she keep that frilly dress clean?" Georgette breathed into Walt's ear. "The hem'll be black as mud."

"Please be quiet," he begged.

He closed his eyes, opened them, breathed and breathed. Soon Philadelphia and a young soldier had fallen in love. When the soldier declared his intentions to marry her, the colonel would not look him in the eye. Philadelphia's face was full of anguish, and a screw in Walt's heart tightened.

"Went riding once and now they's getting married?" Georgette whispered. "This show's just silly."

Two rows behind Walt, Lonnie and Frances were kissing. Walt reached past Georgette and smacked his brother's elbow.

"I need money for peanuts," he said.

Frances sucked her lip, smoothed her skirt. Lonnie dug a half dollar from his pocket and slapped the coin into Walt's palm. "Take Calvin with you."

John Wayne cantered his horse through a pass lined with Apaches, their fierce faces painted for war. Walt stood and the screen went dark. The crowd catcalled up. Hep punched his thigh. The projector's beam lay warm on Walt's neck, and he knew they'd all been plucked from danger and love, from another time, another place, and set back into this dark, sticky-floored theater, in the heart of nothing much that mattered.

A blue-haired woman named Eloise read a paperback behind a long counter. Calvin pressed his nose to the glass, and Eloise held up a crooked finger. She read half a minute more, then marked her place in the book with a ticket stub. Her eyes were teared over, and she raised them to Walt.

"Never marry an Arabian," she said. "They's hot for the evening, but cold come morning."

"I just want some peanuts and licorice."

"Oh, yes," she said. "Peanuts and licorice."

Eloise shook a paper sack and stirred peanuts under the roasting lamps. Walt moved along the counter to where photos of movie stars were displayed beneath the glass: Roy Rogers in a white hat tilted to match his grin; Robert Mitchum hunched over a campfire; Betty Grable dressed as a saloon singer, showing a long, slender leg and pointing six-shooters in the air.

"Anything else?" Eloise said. A sack of peanuts sat on the counter. Calvin leaned against the glass twirling a licorice whip.

"You got photos of Shirley Temple?"

"Well"—Eloise shuffled down and slid open the back of the counter—"we ought to, I think."

She set a photo album before her, then licked her thumb and turned the stiff pages, stopped on a picture and spun the album to face Walt. The photo was of a little girl singing. She wore a ruffled dress, her hands framing her face as if they were the petals of a flower. He'd meant to see a picture of her as Philadelphia. But there was something in this child's face that recalled the innocence of youth and drew from him a nostalgic pulse of joy.

"How much?" Walt asked.

"Half a dollar."

Walt glanced about the lobby to be sure no one was watching. "Keep the other stuff," he said. "I'll take the picture."

Eloise's nose wrinkled. "That boy's woffed on that candy."

Calvin hugged Walt's leg, licorice swinging from his mouth.

"It's my birthday," Walt said, placing the half dollar on the counter. "I'm seventeen today."

"Well," Eloise said, pondering. She turned to the ticket booth by the entrance and hollered, "Earl!"

The booth opened and out leaned Earl. "What you need?"

"This gentleman wants to purchase a star photograph," she said. "He's short a nickel. He tells me it's his birthday and I'm wondering if that means anything to you."

Earl looked Walt up and down. "How'd you get in here?"

Walt glanced back at the theater doors, heard Indians whooping, rifles popping. "Don't know."

"Didn't buy a ticket from me." Earl approached Walt. "Lester let you in the back?" he said, grabbing Walt by the strap of his overalls. "I'll pluck that sneaky goose." He dragged Walt to the front, crashing him through the glass doors and out to the sidewalk.

Earl stalked back into the lobby, wagging a fist at Eloise, and then Calvin was there at the door. The boy flattened his lips against the glass, giggled, ran off. Earl trailed the boy into the dark theater, then Eloise hurried around the counter and across the lobby. She inched open the door, slid out the photo of Shirley Temple.

"Take it," she said, "and don't say nothing about it."

Walt took it.

"You all right, boy?"

Walt stiffened his lip, trying not to cry. He nodded.

Eloise's eyes were full of doubt. "Well," she said, "have you a fine birthday, child." She turned away and the door clicked closed.

Walt sat on the curb in the marquee's light. Smoke draped a fog over the valley. Lester emerged from the alley and crossed the road toward a maroon Studebaker. Walt tucked the photo of Shirley Temple into his bib and trotted over.

"Hey, Lester," Walt called. "I get a lift?"

Lester spun startled. His eyes were wet, the pocket of his shirt torn dog-eared. He no longer wore his usher's jacket. "Fuck you."

"What's wrong with you?"

Lester spat at Walt's boots.

"Hey now," Walt said. "I got kicked out myself—"

"Fuck you." Lester's chin trembled.

"I didn't do nothing to you."

Lester turned to his car. "Fuck you, queer."

Walt watched him open the door, felt the muscles in his shoulders tighten. "Take it back."

Lester climbed into the car.

Walt blocked the door. "Take it back." He clutched Lester's shirtfront.

Lester was crying. "Fuck you," he mumbled. "Just fuck you."

Walt punched Lester's mouth, felt a tooth give. Lester flopped across the seat. Then slowly sat upright, pulled his feet in over the pedals, started the motor. He gripped the door handle, looked up at Walt. His eyes were glazed. Blood trickled from his lip.

Walt had never hit anybody that way and immediately felt ashamed. "I just wanted a ride." He offered Lester his handkerchief, but Lester wouldn't have it.

Walt stepped back, and Lester closed the door. The car pulled away with its headlights off.

Walt sucked a cut on his knuckle, worried some others felt for him the same disgust and pity he'd felt for Lester. He crossed back over to the theater. Earl sat in the ticket booth eating peanuts. Walt leaned against the *Fort Apache* movie poster. He tugged his fedora low, trying to look tough, glaring at Earl through a circle cut in the glass.

"Suppose you're gonna hire another pansy like Lester to stand at that door?"

Earl cracked a shell. "You ain't so big yourself."

"They's bigger boys, but I'm tough as a cob."

Earl tossed the nuts into his mouth, his mustache shifting as he chewed. "I threw you out pretty easy."

"Let me in and see if you get it done twice."

Earl raised his brows, chuckled. "All right." He nodded. "Job's yours if in five minutes' time you get out whoever else snuck in with you."

"Start the clock, mister."

Earl grinned, showing gold-capped teeth. He stepped from the booth and held the door for Walt, who hastened past him and then Eloise, lost again in her paperback.

Once in the theater, Walt paused to steady himself. He slowed his breathing, watching the screen, where soldiers and ladies paraded in a formal dance, the fort's hall bright and clean and full of music. All Walt had wanted to do tonight was see this movie and forget himself for a while. He hated his brother, always causing trouble, was afraid of him. Walt climbed the stairs and crouched in the aisle.

"This movie ain't for shit," he said into Lonnie's ear.

Lonnie yawned. "Ain't been following it."

"Hep got his truck?"

"Think Hep walked somewhere?"

"Them firemen ought to be gone from that lounge," Walt said. "Think we might find something in them cinders?"

"Like what?"

"Like I don't know. Stuff? A radio or something?"

Philadelphia and the soldier kissed on a dark boardwalk, the din of the party behind them. Light from the screen flecked Lonnie's eyes. He tipped the brim of Walt's hat.

"Hep," he called down the aisle. "We gots to go."

The lounge's sign was lightless. The girls and Calvin kept watch from the truck. Walt wore his new usher's jacket, strolling the burnt and dripping shadows. Everything reeked of smoke, everything wet and black. In the middle of the rubble were a table and chairs, bright orange like poppies in a cave. Walt sat at the table expecting to feel a change, a secret breeze. But it was just a chair, damp in its seat, and he couldn't figure why some things burned while others were spared.

In one corner, Hep and Lonnie were inspecting a heap that was once a jukebox. Hep raised a record, trying to read its label by the moonlight. Smoke grimed the night, the moon low and muzzy.

Walt clambered over bricks, joists, the remnants of an old mahogany bar. An icebox had fallen sideways. He tugged open its door to an acrid spill of alcohol. Picking through the refuse, he found an intact bottle of vodka, a bomb-shaped jug of berry liqueur.

Then Lonnie was calling from down by the lanes, where he and Hep struggled lifting a shelf fallen facedown. Walt hurried over, set aside the booze, and grabbed and pulled until the shelf stood upright. Hidden beneath were the wet shining spheres of bowling balls.

Hep lifted a ball. "What we gonna do with 'em?"

Lonnie held a ball swirled blue and white and melted flat on one side. He squinted, peering into its finger holes. "You hear about that girl from Selma?"

"The one that boy Elmer keeps talking up?" Hep asked. "The one what's gonna be in the movies?"

"She singing up in the city?"

"At that pageant?"

"That's tonight, ain't it?"

"We ain't goin' to no goddamn pageant."

"Hell no," said Lonnie, sliding his fingers into the ball. "We goin' to Selma."

Lonnie and Walt rode in the truck bed with the bowling balls. The back roads were pocked, and the balls caromed against the sidewalls. Walt and Lonnie laughed, warding them off with their boot heels. Then Hep turned onto Old Saints Highway, and the balls settled into a languid clatter.

"Lonnie?" Walt said.

Lonnie sat beside him, the vodka in his lap, his eyes shut to the night. "Yep?"

"When we goin' out west?"

Lonnie's eyes didn't open, but he uncapped the bottle. "Hell if I know."

"You said we would when I got old enough. Said one of these times we'd hop a freight and get on out of here."

Lonnie drank, saying nothing.

Walt glanced through the cab's back window. Calvin lay sucking his fingers, asleep in his mama's lap. "I ain't a kid no more."

Lonnie's eyes opened. He wiped the bottle on his sleeve, handed it to Walt. "Won't be no different out there, kid. Out west you ain't got no people to look after you. I'll fight to the bone for you. But not out there. Ain't nobody to fight for you out there."

Vodka burned down Walt's throat. His eyes watered. "All I ever think about is hopping that freight."

Lonnie took back the bottle. "Ever hear of an animal what chews off its leg to get free from a trap?" He set the bottle against his lips. "That's what it's like to try and leave this place. Just ask Hep if my word don't rate."

The road did not buckle or sway, the highway lines unfurling like ropes tethered to town. "I ain't gonna live in no trap," Walt said. "I'm gonna be gone."

"Can't run with but one leg, kid."

Lonnie hooked his arm around Walt's neck and pulled him to lie against his chest. Walt's head rested over his brother's heart, and he watched the dark fields pass, the bowling balls buzzing, tires humming over the pavement.

They trolled between rows of lightless homes, then the road opened onto the square. Three sides were shops with common walls and blond brick facades. Storefront windows gathered moonlight. In the center was a circle of flowers surrounding a copper statue of a soldier, weathered green and glowing like a spirit. They drove past it all and turned up a hill, parking at the crest, the Macy Funeral Home with its white stone belfry shining to the east.

Walt's mind was clear but his legs were drunk. Lonnie unlatched the tailgate. He wiped a ball clean and walked to the middle of the road. They left Calvin sleeping in the cab, the girls and Hep stinking of berry liqueur.

The asphalt gleamed into the square. Lonnie rushed forward and heaved. The ball hopped, bounding higher, accruing velocity, and at the base of the hill slammed square into the passenger door of a long black Chevy.

The others laughed and howled. Walt worried, waiting for a light to turn on in the town.

"It's yours, kid," Lonnie said to Walt. "For your birthday. What you gonna call it?"

"Call what?"

"Your town. Ain't no one here but us."

"Where they at?"

"Up in the city."

"The whole town?"

"Don't take much for these yokels."

Walt surveyed in all directions. "That girl must sing like an angel."

"I heard she sang so pretty it made a man mess his pants," Frances said. "Didn't want to miss a note of her singing and just let loose right there in the hall."

"Hep sings better than that girl," Lonnie said. "Hep's singing'll make you weep."

"Bet that man who shit his pants did some weeping." Frances laughed.

Lonnie scowled. "What the hell you know about anything?"

"I know that girl's goin' off to California to be in the movies, and you and Hep ain't never gonna leave that freight yard and ain't never gonna be nothing."

"Ain't no girl," Lonnie said. "Ain't no freight yard. No Selma. No California. It's all gone. No pageant, no city, no nothing. Ain't nobody but us. We's the only ones left in the whole goddamn world." He glanced over at Walt. "It's your world, brother," he said. "Now what you gonna call it?"

"I don't know."

"Call it how you feel."

Walt peered out over the hot empty land. "Fort Apache," he finally said. "Let's call it Fort Apache."

Walt's ball knocked a puff of brick grain from the First National Bank. Frances shoved her ball from between her legs, and it veered off into the ditch weeds. Hep threw with a hop and a high arm finish and broke the glass of a barber pole, and Georgette's ball launched from a gutter to clang against the statue of the soldier.

In a lull between crashes, Walt sat in the truck beside Calvin, the boy asleep with a ball clutched to his chest, his eyes flitting beneath their lids. Walt couldn't remember what he'd dreamt as a child. But he knew he could never go back to sleeping. Could never be a child again. His whole life now he'd be awake to feelings a child couldn't know.

He covered the boy with his usher's jacket, then pulled from his overalls the photo of Shirley Temple. Her smiling face was perfect. Perfectly asleep. Walt wished he'd never seen her as Philadelphia, kissing soldiers. He laid the photo beside Calvin's cheek.

Sleep, child, he thought, and don't never wake up.

Walt threw ball after ball, knocked the slats off a wooden bench, cracked veins in the market's window, detonated a hubcap off the Chevy's wheel. Glass shrapnel glinted on the sidewalks. Balls dotted the square like a town bombarded by cannon.

Soon the truck bed was empty. Without waking the boy, Lonnie eased the last ball from Calvin's arms. It shone like black glass, a gold star etched around the finger holes.

"Hollywood special," Lonnie said, offering it to Walt.

Walt sank his fingers through the star. He bolted forward and hurled, and shortly came the clatter of glass from the dress shop window in the rear of the square. Hep yawped like a cowboy. Lonnie tore down the hill, and Walt followed, howling, his arms swimming, and Lonnie was far ahead and plucked a ball from a gutter and heaved it through the barbershop's door. Then the road flattened and Walt lost his feet and flopped into the flower beds at the base of the copper soldier.

Walt watched Georgette run by, hair loose in her face. She chucked a ball off her thigh and through the bakery's window. Hep climbed onto the hood of a Buick, slammed a ball against its roof. The post office windows were laced with wire and Frances tossed the same ball, again and again, until the glass folded like a frozen blanket.

Walt took his feet. A copper face, bearded and stern, glowered above him. The soldier did not carry a rifle, but instead an enormous book lay open in its hands. Lonnie called for Walt from inside the dress shop. Walt stared up into the soldier's face. Beneath a short-billed cap its eyes blazed, transfixed on the book. Walt grabbed an unbending arm and lifted himself. But the pages were unreadable, weathered smooth and corroded. He ran his fingers over the cool metal, musing how someday this statue would be gone, and all these buildings and all these roads.

The square was momentarily still. Then Lonnie hollered his name again, and Walt dropped to the ground and raced across the road and the sidewalk of shattered glass.

Inside the dress shop, Lonnie was nude but for a white bonnet, strutting with a hand on his hip and Frances on his arm in a pink fringed dress. Hep skipped ahead of them, tossing panties as a flower girl would petals. Georgette swayed naked before a trifold mirror, slow-dancing. Then Frances was beside Walt, laughing, saying she needed a bridesmaid, pulling a dress over his head. Her laughter was warm but Walt didn't laugh and off came his fedora.

She tossed it to Lonnie and stretched a wig over Walt's skull.

Lonnie ran with the fedora, chasing Georgette. She shrieked, pale breasts bobbing, then Frances's face was in front of Walt's saying, "You're so beautiful, Walt," and Walt didn't want Georgette to wear his hat and ran after Lonnie through the racks of dresses.

Clothes smacked Walt's shoulders and face. He ran desperate but couldn't catch his brother, on through the back and toward the front washed in milky moonlight. Glass crunched beneath Walt's boots and he suddenly felt light-headed, as if he might be sick. He bent at the waist, gasping.

When he stood again he faced the mirror. Walt saw himself in triplicate, in this wig blond and curled in a popular style. He regarded his dirty face in the faintly reflected light, his furrowed brow. He looked older, looked like a film star.

Then Hep stood behind him. He lifted off the wig, slapped the fedora onto Walt's head. Light flashed in the back and Hep looked away. Walt looked, too, to see Lonnie running, yelping, twirling a burning dress above his head. Its hem threw sparks, the flames brighter with each turn. Walt turned again to his reflection, saw Hep gazing solemnly at him. Their eyes held each other in the mirror.

Hep slugged Walt's shoulder. "Wanna ring the bell?"

They ran whooping across the square, past the soldier and the bank and the ruined Chevy. Climbing the hill, Walt shed the frock and hurled it into the weeds. He followed Hep through a ditch and the funeral home's yard to stand beneath a dark window. Palms on the pane, Hep pushed and the window lifted.

"Give me a boost," he said.

Walt clasped his fingers, and Hep stepped into them and climbed through the window.

Walt grabbed the sill, pulled himself up. He tumbled inside and into Hep, knocking him down. Hep groaned and then was on Walt, and they rose laughing, knocking aside folding chairs, shoving, tackling each other.

They found stairs leading up and took them. Hep grabbed Walt in a headlock, and Walt laughed, trying to keep his feet. Then came another flight of stairs, narrow and lightless. They climbed blindly, Walt clutching the back of Hep's belt. Then Hep was saying *hold it, hold it*. After some fumbling, a door swung open, and sterling light flooded the stairwell.

They scampered into the belfry, an octagonal room open to the night. In the middle hung an enormous glowing bell, its metal reflecting the moonlight. Hep was sweating. His smile had vanished, his eyes searching Walt's face as he unbuttoned his shirt.

Hep's chest was wormed with scars. Drawn above the palpitations of his actual heart was a blue ink tattoo of a heart—not a cartoon heart, but an organ twisted and muscular, arteries jutting like snakes strangling a stone. He grasped Walt's arm and lurched to the sill and Walt thought they might jump, was relieved when Hep stopped short.

"Ain't it like a movie?" Hep said, softly.

They were eye level with the moon, brightly haloed. A silver lacquer lay over the town's many roofs.

"Ever feel like your mind's set funny?" Hep said. "Like ain't a person in the world could understand you? I think I'm crazy. I really think I must be." Walt watched Hep's face, flushed in mercurial light. "Sometimes I wish I was in the movies," he said. "Not to be famous or nothing. I just wish I was made of light. Then nobody'd know me except for what they saw up on that screen. I'd just be light up on the silver screen, and not at all a man."

Walt's ears grew hot. "I'm gonna leave someday," he said. "Goin' out west. You could come with if you want." His voice was eager, unsure. "We could look out for each other."

Walt heard voices down in the road, Lonnie and the girls wildly calling for them to come on. Moonlight poured over Hep. "It don't matter," Hep said, tears collecting in his broken eye. "Stay or go, it's all the same. Went overseas to kill boys who weren't like me 'cause them boys hated others who weren't like them, neither. What that change? Put a black boy in that lounge, or one of them Jews, and see how it goes. Don't care what Lonnie says. Burn a thousand bowling alleys, burn up the whole goddamn world, ain't nothing gonna change."

Walt followed Hep's gaze out beyond the square to a long row of headlights approaching from the highway. Lonnie and the girls stood half-dressed in the funeral home yard, hollering for them to come on, that they had to get the hell out of there.

Walt stared into Hep's tearing eye. He wiped Hep's cheek with his palm. "What's it all for then?"

Hep shrank away, turned to slump against the gleaming bell.

Then Walt didn't want to believe Hep, desperately wanted to go back to how they'd been. "We gonna ring the bell, Hep?" he asked, trying to sound cheerful.

Hep struck the soft of his fist against the bell.

"Maybe we should ring it?"

Hep lay his face in his hands.

"Should we, Hep?"

Hep's head lolled from side to side.

"Won't never get another chance."

THE DAUGHTER

1

Miriam lifted her face from the tabletop. She squinted, the sun glaring through the kitchen window. Pastor Hamby pulled out a chair and sat across from her, his eyes turned to the wall. The wallpaper was dingy white, a pattern of roosters and tractors and shocks of wheat, once red, now faded brown. Behind the pastor stood the sheriff, Helen Farraley, a big woman dressed head to toe in tan.

"How many?" Miriam said.

"Witnesses?" the sheriff asked.

Miriam nodded. Her daughter, Evelyn, stood like a sentinel at her side, caressing her hand.

The sheriff leaned back against the cupboards, held her jacket closed at her throat. "Staties got accounts from thirteen."

"And none helped?"

"It happened fast, Miriam."

"Not a single one to help an old woman?"

The sheriff stared at the floor, rubbed the back of her neck.

The pastor reached across the table and squeezed Miriam's wrist. "Birdie," he said. "I been thinking about something that plagued me back when I was starting out. About Christ carrying that cross to Calvary." His eyes set upon her. "I mean, he had these disciples and all these followers, right? Folks who loved him, who thought he was the Messiah? And not one of them took up for him. Nobody fought for him. Not really." The pastor lifted a salt shaker shaped like a rooster, but the bottom was loose and salt trickled out and he set it back down. "For a long time I wondered what that said about people." He brushed at the salt on the table. "But then I realized it was just meant that way, what with Jesus up on that cross alone. God put fear in brave hearts and froze 'em over."

An arc of salt, where the pastor's hand had passed, remained on the table. "She die fast?" Miriam asked to the room.

The sheriff made a noise in her throat. "Probably didn't see him at all. She didn't turn, we know that."

"All for a shitty truck."

The sheriff shut her eyes a moment. "He was trying to get away, went after the first car he saw."

Miriam pressed her daughter's fingers to her lips, then pushed out her chair and stood. "What's to happen now?"

The sheriff stood away from the cupboards. "There'll be a trial," she said. "Waste of time, you ask me. Guy was high as a kite, been in and out of prison his whole life. A dozen witnesses, security cameras from the supermarket." She hung her thumbs on her gun belt. "Let me have him, is what I say."

Miriam crossed to the sink, stared out the window. Down the hill, in the valley beneath the house, the corn rows spread shin-high and green, the leaves gleaming sunlight.

"If I was there," Miriam said, without turning, "I'd of fought for Jesus. They'd of had to kill me. I'd of been but teeth and nails once they got me turned off."

2

High pale stalks drooped against the heat as Miriam strolled the maze she'd had cut in her corn. Blackbirds mewling, the air reeking of the field, she blotted her neck with a bandanna and wondered what her mother would've thought of this maze. Miriam knew she'd disapprove, but it'd been a rough year, and they had plenty of money from Mama's insurance, so what did it matter, after all they'd been through, her mother three months deceased and the trial soon to start, if Miriam simply wanted to get lost for a while, to take long dawdling strolls away from the world?

A scuttling broke out in the corn. Miriam stopped her stroll, flinched as a small gray terrier and a shaggy mutt burst into the hall. The gray dog paused, eyeing her, panting, then ran off. Miriam wanted to catch them, to pet them. She walked faster, trying to keep them in sight, but the corridor curved and there was only so far she could see.

Miriam thought them gone, when again she heard a rustling. She stood rigid, listening. The movement in the stalks grew near, then they broke into the corridor, the terrier and the mutt, with two young boys grasping at their tails.

The dogs scrabbled into the opposing rows. Upon seeing Miriam, the boys stood as startled wildlife, their bare chests heaving, their hair tangled, faces filthy. The older was maybe twelve, the younger a half-sized twin of his brother.

These were the McGahees, who lived with their father, Seamus, a sharecropper who worked a spat of land just down the road. That past July, the boys had shot bottle rockets at cars, blew up mailboxes all along Old Saints Highway, Miriam's included.

"You ain't allowed here," Miriam hollered, stalking toward them.

They fled, their skinny arms pumping. Instinct told Miriam to chase them down and put them straight, but her legs felt wooden as she plodded over the uneven ground. The boys' boots blurred in the dust. Their bodies grew small. One path split into two, and when Miriam arrived at the fork they were gone. The right path ended in a blunt wall of crop. But the left ran a slender curve into the sunlit expanse of the maze's center.

Miriam rushed toward the light. Each step licked fire up her shins. Huffing, she burst into the clearing. Here the crop lay open in a circle twenty yards wide, with corridors shooting off the center like spokes from a hub. Across the rotunda, in the mouth of a hall, she glimpsed the hunched outlines of boys.

Miriam took a hard step in their direction, but a hand yanked her arm. She shrieked, whirled.

It was Evelyn. "I was calling after you," she said. "Didn't you hear me?" The girl stared into her eyes as might a doctor. "What you running from? Why you running from me?"

Miriam struggled to catch her breath. She glanced past Evelyn to the far corridor. The boys were gone. She tried not to cry, tried to stay strong for her daughter.

"Oh, come now," Evelyn pleaded, clutching Miriam's hand. "Everything's fine, Mama. Everything'll be just fine."

Miriam sat before the vanity, gazed into the mirror and up at Evelyn, who stood behind her and brushed her hair. Twenty-one and fresh as rain, Evelyn had gone a year to the nursing college, still had an apartment in the city. Miriam told her she was free to go back, and now wondered why she stayed. Duty, she guessed. Pity, more likely.

"Let's not be sad, Mama," Evelyn cooed.

Miriam's spine was a kinked wire. She shrugged.

"Can't let them boys get you down." Evelyn lay the brush on the table and picked up the eyeliner. "Come on," she urged, with a grin. "Close your eyes and look up at me."

"How can I look at you with my eyes closed?"

Evelyn shook the pencil at her. "I'll pinch you, I swear."

Miriam gave a grunt, but shut her eyes and tilted her head.

"What we need is a monster for our maze," Evelyn said, and Miriam felt the pencil marking her brows. "A monster to gobble up little boys."

Soon the pencil stopped, and Miriam opened her eyes to her own reflection, a menacing angular brow, eyes darkly shaded.

Miriam groaned a laugh.

"There's that smile." Evelyn kissed her mother's head. "Now let's have us a nap, and I'll plan something special. An evening for a thousand smiles."

Miriam woke from a troublesome dream, a scene of being stuck in a tree's high branches, some unseen menace approaching, the mutt and the terrier frantically barking from the ground below, but she was too weak, too scared, to climb down. She rubbed her eyes, sat upright. Late-afternoon light slanted over the bed. As the dream's feeling lingered, Miriam considered she might still be asleep.

Slowly she rose and wandered downstairs and out onto the porch. This was no dream. The valley was a maze, five acres of spirals looping like swine tails out to where the field met the knobs, like a doily had been draped over the land.

The screen door bumped open and out stepped Evelyn. Her giggling face was painted with rouge, her nose black with mascara.

Miriam spat a laugh. "Good lord, child."

Evelyn laughed, too, her teeth absurdly white against her brown lips. "Now we're just a couple of monsters," she said, and gave Miriam's shoulder a squeeze. "Get your bearings, then get on your shoes. I've got such a surprise for you, Mama."

They carried baskets filled with candles, the good china, a chicken roasted with rosemary, spinach and strawberry salad, and two bottles of red wine. They followed the trail of twine Evelyn had unfurled while Miriam slept, the string snaking through the stubble, around bends and swags, all the way to the center.

In the rotunda, beneath the open dusky sky, sat a table with a white linen cloth. Miriam whistled and applauded as Evelyn lit tall white candles. They laughed and sipped wine. They had forgotten utensils, so Miriam tore strips of chicken with her fingers, plucked strawberries, one by one, from the salad. Evening gathered in the valley. Evelyn's painted face grew dark. When the meal was done, Miriam was full and giddy and more than a little drunk.

The crop whispered, the corn swaying. Evelyn blew out the candles, pulled a radio from the basket and played an old bouncy tune Miriam loved. The sky hung a black cloth sprinkled with luminous dust. Miriam felt as if filled with the gentle breeze. She pulled Evelyn from her chair and together they laughed and danced in the field.

Miriam woke on a pallet of blankets. Through the morning mist, she watched the terrier lick plates up on the table. The black mutt was curled at her feet, its snout tucked into its belly. Miriam nudged Evelyn beside her and together they smiled at the dogs.

With scraps of chicken, Miriam lured the dogs back through the maze. The happiness from the night before remained. The mist gave way to a sterling sun, and Miriam decided she'd always have a maze. Would keep the dogs.

She named the terrier Pip, the black dog Wooly. On the house's shaded porch, Miriam set out bowls of water. They left the dogs while Evelyn went to shower, and Miriam packed a basket for a picnic. But when Miriam returned to the porch to toss the dogs some chunks of ham, they were gone.

Miriam whistled for them, searched all about the hillside, walked her little barn, calling. But they didn't show themselves. She stared back up at the house, wondering if Evelyn had finished changing, then heard voices down in the corn, a dog yelping.

She followed the noise into the field, raced in a frenzy down a corridor, peeking down the halls she passed. Then she saw them, the littlest McGahee awkwardly trying to carry Pip, his older brother, a quiver on his back and a hunting bow slung across his chest, slashing at Wooly with a metal arrow.

Miriam rushed toward them. The little boy dropped Pip and scurried into the rows. The older stood defiant, brandishing the arrow like a sword. Miriam pounced, yanked the arrow from his fist, and began to thrash his legs. The boy shrieked, holding out his hands as Miriam lashed his wrists, his shoulders. She heard Evelyn shouting but didn't stop, and then the boy whirled free, welts striping his back as he dashed into the corn.

Then Evelyn was behind her, easing the arrow from her grip. The field and sky slowly spun. Miriam stood gasping, adrift in her own shuddering body, her own reeling mind.

"Just leave," she sobbed. "Why don't you just leave me?"

Evelyn shook Miriam once. "Stop it, Mama. You're not the only one in this, you know."

They didn't speak the entire way back to the house. The hill seemed an endless climb. Miriam entered the shade of the house, wandered upstairs into her bathroom, and closed the door. As she passed the mirror she flinched at her reflection. The makeup was faded, smeared, but still remained from the night before. Miriam had forgotten about her face. What a sight she must've been.

She sat on the edge of the bathtub, holding her head. She eyed the little pink bath mat, wanting to go to sleep. But she could not lie on the floor, couldn't rise, either, and then the door inched open, and Evelyn poked in her head.

She sat beside Miriam, took her mother gently by the shoulders. "Let's have some lunch, Mama," she said. "You'll feel better with some food in you."

Miriam nodded.

"Want a sandwich?"

Miriam trembled. "My face," she softly cried.

They sat still, Evelyn holding Miriam tight. Then Evelyn crouched before her, her hands on her mother's knees. "I'll make up my face, too," she said, smirking. "Just to be silly. We'll find those boys and scare them off for good."

The twinkle in Evelyn's eyes was contagious, made Miriam chuckle. She leaned down and kissed her daughter's hands.

They ate sandwiches on the porch, Miriam's energy restored, her spirits lifted. Evelyn made them over, painting her mother's face, then her own, both donning red masks with black-ringed eyes, gold hoop earrings hung from black noses.

They strolled the maze, arm in arm, laughing, singing improvised songs about monsters gobbling children. At the field's farthest edge, an outbuilding's aluminum roof peaked above the corn. Miriam pushed through the rows. Evelyn squeezed Miriam's elbow, asked what she was doing. Miriam shushed Evelyn and pointed.

Over by the outbuilding stood a hickory tree, and from the tree hung a hammock in which Samuel Franklin slept. Samuel was

Miriam's oldest neighbor, had been her mother's dear friend. They trod softly to his side, his legs dangled over the hammock's ropes, his eyes twitching beneath their thin wrinkled lids.

A charcoal grill sat a few feet away. Miriam tiptoed over, quietly took out a briquette. She rubbed her hands black with the coal, then hurried back to Samuel. Gently, she dragged a finger across his forehead. Samuel didn't budge, and Miriam held her breath to keep from laughing.

Soon Samuel's nose, neck, even his ears, were black. They leaned their faces above his. Miriam brusquely shook his arm. Samuel's eyes opened halfway, then he saw them and let out a little hoot, his arms flailing, and the hammock swung and Samuel flopped to the dirt.

They fled cackling like schoolgirls, tears in Miriam's eyes and corn leaves slapping her face as she rushed into the rows. But then her eyes were stinging. Her lungs strained. She coughed, couldn't breathe, couldn't see for the tears and corn. Miriam stumbled, reaching, grasping at the stalks.

Then Evelyn stood above her, sweat dripping rouge down the girl's throat. Evelyn held her hand, hollered for Samuel. Soon Samuel's black-coated face hovered above her, too. He gawked a moment, saying nothing, then cradled Miriam up into his arms.

Miriam lay held in the hammock. Evelyn pressed two fingers to her mother's wrist and wouldn't let her rise. Samuel stood beside her, his cracked old face dusted with charcoal.

"Think I understand some things now," he said.

"Things?" Miriam asked.

He scratched under his collar. "This morning I saw Seamus McGahee in town. Hardly spoke to the man in my life, and here he comes over saying his boys saw devils in your field. Devils drinking and dancing."

Miriam pushed away her daughter's hand, struggled to raise herself upright. *"Devils?"*

"What he said."

"And what you say?"

"Thought the man lost his mind." His eyes turned inward. "Didn't know you all were out there that way."

Miriam grabbed Evelyn's elbow and swung her legs out of the hammock to stand.

"Miriam?"

"What?" she said, crossly.

"You're kicking the beehive." Samuel tapped a boot heel against the ground. "All this crazy stuff's got folks talking. What with your mama's passing and you so out of sorts."

"I'm no devil," she barked.

His eyes bulged white upon his sooted face. "Folks are talking just the same."

"Your face is filthy, Samuel," she said, like a slap, then tugged Evelyn's hand and stomped off through the yard.

Miriam sulked as they worked their chores, doing laundry, dishes, cleaning the bathrooms. When she found Evelyn in her bedroom, changing her sheets, Miriam made her stop. Evelyn begged that they sleep in the house, but Miriam was adamant. It was her land. She'd not be told what to do.

That evening after dinner, their faces washed clean, they returned to the rotunda with a cooler of snacks, a jug of water, and citronella candles. The events of the day had left Miriam weary, yet sleep came in vexed shreds, mosquitoes buzzing her ears, the moon ducking in and out of the clouds. Deep in the night, Evelyn sleeping soundly beside her, Miriam could no longer lie stewing.

Since her mother's death she often walked at night. Mostly, she'd paced the dark house. Sometimes stepped onto the porch. Once, she'd gone out into the drive and stared long at their old Ford. The truck that had been impounded as evidence. The truck from which they'd washed her mother's blood.

Tonight her hands shook as she laced her boots, lost in the throes of a more desperate ache, an unsettled yearning to be apart from all things human. Miriam chose a corridor and pushed into the maze. She marched through the dark, Samuel's words roiling in her mind. It was always the same. The same prattling voices, same narrow judgments. The world was the same, though Miriam had changed. She knew what they wanted. They wanted the old Miriam. Miriam in the choir loft, Miriam bringing chili to the potluck, Miriam judging rabbits at the fair.

But how could she abide? No, she seethed. That Miriam is gone. I can't go back. Now she'd demand gratitude. Demand notice that she, too, would soon leave them. Any day, any moment. She wanted them to mourn her now, wanted to be missed before her blood stained some parking lot's asphalt.

A fever wrenched through her, tightening her spine, the cords of her throat. She felt like screaming and would've had she not wanted to chance waking Evelyn. Clouds covered the moon. Blindly she bumped along, her hand trailing along the wall of crop. Then the ground sloped downward. She paused to find her footing.

Miriam heard something. A breaking in the swale.

She crouched, one hand clutching a stalk, her entire mind lit as she peered down into the darkness. Something was there. Her breathing quickened. A vein in her neck throbbed. Maybe it's one of the dogs, Miriam told herself, trying to steady her nerves.

She softly whistled, patted her thigh.

The land lay still.

Miriam inched down the slope, squinting to see. It was there. She could see it. An obscure hump. Again she whistled, reached out.

The thing exploded in a flurry. She was struck. Miriam fell onto her back, was hit again, and she threw out her hands, the thing thrashing over her. She caught a thin arm. Ripped something cold and hard from its grip, and lashed out, the impact, like an ax breaking pond ice, reverberating through her arm.

Miriam scrambled back up the rise. She heard nothing but her own burning breaths. Nothing came after her, nothing moving down in the darkness. She recognized she held a section of pipe, and let it fall from her fist.

She flexed the elbow that'd been struck, staggered along the corridor. When she found the center, wispy clouds veiled the night, the rotunda hazed in sepia moonlight. Evelyn slept on her back, her mouth slightly open, both dogs curled beside her. Miriam found herself suddenly exhausted. Gingerly, she lay down beside her daughter and closed her eyes.

3

Dawn fanned its pale light over the field. Miriam stirred slowly, the mutt snuggled heavily against her. She turned her eyes to Evelyn, asleep beside her, and wondered what Evelyn would do once she was dead, what residue of her life she'd leave behind.

Miriam began to hum an old hymn. Today was Sunday. She'd not been to church since her mother's funeral, but she missed it, she realized, the nice clothes, the bells and the singing, and the lull after the organ's song when all bowed their heads and took silent accounting of themselves.

She stroked Evelyn's cheek. The girl's eyes batted open, squinting in the sunlight.

"Wake up, hon," Miriam whispered, shading her daughter's eyes. "I need to sing today. Need those lovely old songs."

They followed the twine back through the maze. Miriam caught Evelyn glancing at her arm. Miriam said nothing, tried to let her arm swing naturally.

"Why you walking like that?" her daughter finally asked. Evelyn stopped her, raised her sleeve. "Oh, Mama," she said, passing a finger over, but not touching, the deep bruise across the back of her arm. "That from when you fell?"

Miriam didn't answer.

"You need a doctor?"

Miriam eased down her sleeve. "You'll take good enough care of me, won't you, hon?" she asked Evelyn.

Her daughter's brow furrowed, her eyes intently studying Miriam's face. "You're my mama," she said. "What else would I do?"

They took the little car Miriam bought Evelyn for school. The sun already blazed, the heat wavering over the road. Miriam tried to breathe easy as they passed the end of their corn. Half a mile from there sat the McGahee place, a squat little house, its siding pissed with rust, its yard just weedy dirt and an old truck with high slatted sides. Miriam averted her gaze, feigning nonchalance and humming a tune until they slowed coming into town.

Evelyn rolled down her window. Miriam left hers up. Carts of melons and peaches were on display in front of Freely's, the rest of the strip closed, and they eased up the hill and pulled into the church's lot.

Krafton Baptist was a barn-style chapel with a high white steeple. Much of the town belonged as members, and this morning the pews were full. Faces turned as Miriam and Evelyn walked the side aisle, some smiling, others standing, reaching to shake Miriam's hand. A murmur flitted through the sanctuary, Miriam nodding at folks, her hurt arm braced against her.

They sat in the third pew from the front, in what had been their usual spot beside Doctor Peterson, a bent old man in large black-rimmed glasses. He was retired now, but had been her mother's doctor, her grandmother's, as well.

"Well, I'll be," he said, soft and hoarse.

Miriam forced a smile.

"Good to see you," he said. "Been too long, sister."

Evelyn sat on the other side of Miriam. Sunshine through the stained-glass cast blue jeweled light over her. Miriam wished she was as gracious as her daughter, who'd run interference all this time, keeping the world at bay, taking the phone calls, greeting the well-wishers, as Miriam lay in bed with the shades drawn.

The organ burst into song. The congregation rose, and Pastor Hamby, a huge man in a red satin robe, ambled from the back of the sanctuary and up onto the dais.

"Peace be with you," he said, holding high his Bible.

"*Peace,*" Miriam repeated, with the congregation.

Samuel Franklin stood in the front pew with the other deacons. Evelyn nudged Miriam and whispered for her to look at his neck. Charcoal smudges showed behind each ear. Evelyn giggled and Miriam whispered for her to hush.

Pastor Hamby preached from Second Thessalonians, a warning against idleness and being a burden onto others. "If a man will not work," he boomed, "he shall not eat. To be concerned with the birth of a universe," he said, dabbing his brow with a handkerchief, "is to divert from the birth of God, a seed taking root in the soil, a crop growing from pebbles then cutting it to a weasel's shadow to feed the masses."

His sermon ended with one of his poetic diatribes, charging that we not hide from God, but seek his face in the stars.

"Scientists say our universe is expanding," he said. "And I'm fine with that. After all, would God's universe be shrinking? So let's think of pancake batter poured into a skillet, spreading to its edges. If our universe is spreading like batter, then what's the skillet? I'm not a brilliant man. But I am a curious man. And I'm not afraid of questions, for all answers lead back to Him." He pointed a finger skyward. "My faith's in knowing the edges of our universe are the upturned palms of a benevolent God."

Miriam imagined a palm filled with pancake batter. As the pastor said amen and the choir broke into "The Old Rugged Cross," she could not find her voice to sing.

The deacons circulated the offering plates. When Samuel waited at the end of their row, Miriam watched his eyes. He glanced at her and scratched his neck. Before stepping to the next pew, he leaned forward, and whispered, "You two ought to grow up."

The congregation released into the churchyard, folding tables set out for fellowship, kids playing kickball down in the willows. Everybody swarmed Miriam, saying how good it was to see her. Minny Tollefson said there was a hole in every song without her voice in the choir. Kelsy Upton invited them to a barbeque next Friday, to swim in their lake, play some bridge. Miriam drifted through them all, a bit bleary, like a curtain had been opened and she was suddenly onstage.

Walt Freely, mayor of Krafton and owner of the diner and grocery store, waved Miriam over. He sat, gray haired and frail, beside

Doctor Peterson in the shade of an elm tree. His hand, shaking and spotted, took hold of Miriam's fingers.

"Heard you cut a maze in your corn," he said.

"Yes, sir."

"How's that?"

"Yes, sir," Miriam said, louder.

He smiled. "I'll bring the little 'uns out to see it."

"No," she said, more firmly than she intended.

He sat back a little.

She softened her tone. "It's not for the public, Mr. Freely."

He turned an ear to her. "How's that?"

"It's just for us," she said, louder, trying to smile.

"I see." He patted her hand. "Well, if there's anything you need from the store, just call and we'll bring it on out. The peaches are a wonder. Marilyn just made some pies. I want you to have one."

She looked into his old eyes and wondered what he really thought, what he'd say once she was out of earshot. "Thank you," she said. "I'll stop and get one."

A heavy arm dropped around her shoulders and there stood Pastor Hamby, in the brown western suit he often wore. "Lost chickadee's come to roost," he said. "How's my Birdie?"

The smiling man, sweating and his cheeks red from the sun, looked as if he'd worked a day in the fields.

"Pastor," Miriam said, "I need to speak with you."

They stood within the shade of a willow tree, kids shrieking, playing ball just beyond the curtain of branches. Pastor Hamby stood before Miriam, bits of sunlight dappling his shoulders as he hunched beneath the limbs. "Been worried about you," he said. "We all have."

Miriam couldn't look at him square.

"Stopped by a few times. I'm sure Evelyn told you."

The sun flashing through the ropy boughs, Miriam felt a tremor of nausea. "What you said about questions," she blurted. She balled her fists, inhaled.

A red ball bounded beneath the branches and against Miriam's leg. A boy, his white shirt untucked from his suit pants, burst in. The child jumped, startled, regarding them. Then he grabbed up the ball and dashed back out. Miriam eyed the spot where the boy had passed, watched the shadows of limbs sway in the dirt.

The pastor touched her elbow. "Why don't you come tomorrow? We'll go to the diner, have the whole morning to talk."

Miriam's mind whirled.

"What do you say, Birdie?"

She cradled her arm, struggling to gather her mind.

Pastor Hamby began to say something more. He tried a smirk. "We'd best get from under this tree before folks think we're necking." The pastor's face fell grave. He glanced off through the branches toward the noise of the children.

Miriam nodded, releasing a long-held breath.

Miriam remained under the willow, fortifying herself. She pinched color back into her cheeks and rushed out, smiling at the kids playing ball, smiling as she passed through the tables, complimenting Janice Walters on her dress, telling Dona Jankovich her voice sounded lovely during the hymns. All along she scanned about for Evelyn, and found her talking to Samuel in the chapel's vestibule.

Miriam smiled at Evelyn, at Samuel and Ed Macon, another deacon. She pulled a tissue from her handbag. "Your mama not teach you to wash behind your ears?" she said, and dabbed the smudges on Samuel's neck.

Ed Macon laughed. "Take the farmer from the field, but can't take the field from the farmer."

Samuel pointed at Miriam. "I'm gonna get you."

Miriam playfully swatted his finger.

"I invited Samuel for a picnic," Evelyn said. "A peace offering."

Miriam's heart lurched. "Oh, no. Not today, hon."

"Mama." Evelyn gave her a look to say she was being rude.

"I'm sorry," she said to Samuel. "I'm just tired is all."

"Well, I invited him, so do what you want, but he's coming. Isn't that right, Samuel?"

Samuel grinned. "Can't argue with the nurse."

They stopped at Freely's General. Miriam hadn't been there in months, tried to relax while picking out a peach pie. The girl at the check-stand, in her black nails and lipstick, who'd worked there for years and whom Miriam felt she knew though she'd never spoken to her beyond the transaction at hand, stared at Miriam. Miriam suspected what she wanted. Photos of her mother had gotten out on the Internet, the truck door splattered, her mother facedown on the asphalt. Girls like her were curious about such things.

"I like your nails," Miriam told her.

The girl didn't blink. "You want your lottery ticket?"

"No," Miriam told her. "Thank you, sweetie, but I don't play that anymore."

Samuel stood waiting on the porch. He carried the peach pie while Evelyn hauled the picnic basket, and Miriam a pitcher of tea. They followed the twine through the maze. As long as they followed the twine, Miriam figured everything would be okay. But then they turned a corner and there, far down the hall, strolled the older McGahee boy. He wore a yellow T-shirt, the longbow in his fist, the dogs at his heels.

"*Boy!*" Miriam shouted.

The dogs turned, bounded happily back toward Miriam. The boy surveyed them all, then darted away.

"Come back here!" she shrieked.

The boy didn't halt.

Samuel called, "McGahee, you stop where you're at."

The boy leered back, slowed to a trot. Samuel handed Evelyn the pie. He said he'd make sure the boy left the field, took off at a jog. Miriam watched the boy near the hall's end, staring hard into the rows, slapping his bow against the stalks he passed.

Twenty minutes later, Samuel returned to the rotunda, said he'd trailed the boy out of the corn and watched him run up Old Saints Highway, said he'd later go talk with the boy's father. They all sat around the table. Miriam's energy had dwindled, her mood somber.

"I used to play the lottery," she said. "Same numbers every week. Dreamed of having so much money I could tell certain folks to go to hell." She locked eyes with Evelyn. "Some dream, huh? I'll bet you'll all be glad when I'm dead and no longer a burden."

Evelyn looked away.

Samuel's suit jacket hung on the seat behind him, and he reached into its breast pocket and retrieved a silver flask. "Hey, nursey," he said to Evelyn. "I give your patient some medicine?"

Evelyn answered without pause. "Give her a double."

Miriam sipped whiskey in her tea and watched the clouds smother the sun. She stroked Wooly, her bones feeling brittle, as if her fingers would break if pressed. A horde of grackles exploded from the field, up into the gray. She watched the birds rise and drift, then dart en masse, as if yanked by invisible wires, down again into the crop.

Samuel squinted at Miriam.

"What?" she asked him.

"Nothing."

"Say what you have to."

He sucked his teeth. "Can still get some feed from this crop. Before the birds get it all."

Miriam shook her head. "It's my land."

"It don't put you in good standing."

"I don't care what the others think."

"No," he said. "Don't put you right with God."

"God?" Miriam chuckled once. "Oh lord, Samuel. I think God's rightly proven me out of his graces."

"Bad things happen to good people."

"And me? You think I'm a good person?"

Samuel eyed his flask on the table. "You've always been kind to me."

"But I'm going to Hell?"

"I didn't say nothing about that."

"But that's what you think?"

"No, ma'am."

"Well, maybe there's not a Heaven and Hell," she said. "Maybe this is all we've got."

The wind hissed through the corn, smelling of rain.

"Shame to waste a crop," Samuel said, shrugging on his suit jacket. "That's all I meant."

A drizzle became a downpour became a storm. Frantically, they gathered what they could and scampered through the maze. The tea pitcher slipped from Miriam's grip, and Evelyn yelled to leave it. They huddled beneath Samuel's jacket, were soaked through by the time they clambered up the hill and under the porch's eaves.

Evelyn ran inside and returned with towels. She gave a towel to Samuel, wrapped one around her mother's neck. "Come get a hot bath," Evelyn said, ruffling the towel over Miriam's hair. "Then we'll get you into bed."

Miriam yanked the towel from Evelyn's hands. "I'm not a child," she snapped. "Get Samuel some dry clothes, and bring me some, too. Samuel's going to stay awhile," she said, loud enough for Samuel to hear at the end of the porch. "We'll play cards and just wait it out together."

Samuel turned from the railing. "McGahee's out there."

Beyond Samuel, the rain overwhelming the gutters fell in a quavering fan, and through the blear Miriam saw the box of rust that was Seamus McGahee's truck at the end of her drive.

Miriam stepped to the porch rail. The green sky hung bearded, the curves of the maze alive, flexing, swelling.

They pulled chairs around the sofa where Miriam lay propped by pillows, played gin rummy. Samuel wore Evelyn's denim work shirt and big gray sweatpants. Between games, he peered out the windows. Rain drummed on the clapboards. The parlor's wainscoting was dark, and though the lamps were on, a gloom resided over them.

"Put on the radio," Miriam told Evelyn.

Evelyn switched on the radio, turning the tuner dial, unable to find anything but static. Miriam hadn't heard his steps on the porch, but saw a figure in orange just outside the screen door. The figure called for Samuel.

Samuel turned to the voice. He looked to Miriam, asking permission. Miriam nodded, and he crossed the room and opened the door. There waited Seamus McGahee, in a hunter's slick and cap, his thick beard and high rubber boots glistening wet.

Miriam clutched her cards to her chest. Samuel asked Seamus to come in, but the man just gazed at his boots.

"My boy's missing," he said. "My oldest says he's in that corn. Says you run him off 'fore he could find his baby brother."

The child was seven. Seamus had been searching for two hours. He stood in the dingy porch light, his eyes seeming to bore through Miriam. Samuel said he'd help look, and stepped onto the porch to grab his jacket and shoes.

Evelyn squeezed Miriam's arm. "Stay here."

Miriam felt as if the storm raged inside her. She pressed a hand to her sternum, said, "Flashlights are in the pantry."

Evelyn ran down the hall and returned with the lights. She held a palm to Miriam's forehead. "Maybe you should just get to bed," Evelyn pleaded, gazing into her mother's eyes. "Please don't be stubborn, Mama," she whispered. "Not tonight."

A nod was all Miriam could manage.

Evelyn kissed Miriam's head, then hurried out on the porch.

Miriam watched through the screen door as Evelyn handed each man a flashlight, then lifted a red poncho over her head. Miriam eyed Seamus McGahee's orange slicker, Samuel's light-gray legs, as the men stepped off the porch and down into the slanting rain.

Miriam lay on the sofa, the rain ticking like pebbles against the windows. Gradually, the storm relented. Unable to rest, Miriam stepped out onto the porch. Wind trickled damp against her cheeks. The air reeked of mud. Water dripping from the eaves was all that moved, the maze steeped in molasses dark. Miriam was sure this was what death would be, dark and quiet and terribly lonesome.

Then she didn't want to be alone. She rushed inside and dressed in her rubber boots and winter parka. She trod slowly, cautiously, down the hillside. Clouds parted to a spattering of stars. Where they'd normally enter the maze, Miriam searched for the twine, but the rain had flushed the grade and it wasn't to be found.

Mud sucked at her heels as she listened for footsteps, for voices. Shivering, she wandered. Hall upon hall, each bowing indistinctly, every selfsame corridor an empty aisle of quiet.

She stumbled upon the rotunda, the little table blown over, blankets strewn about. The rotunda corridors were the mouths of mines uncharted. Miriam picked one, bent a stalk to lean over the gap. If she returned to the center that hall would be marked.

She plodded again into the maze, the halls bending, endlessly looping. Time dripped as rain from her fingers. Her elbow throbbed. The bones of her knees knocked like flint against flint. In her mind, each sparking step was a day removed from her life.

Moonlight glinted off something in the mud. Was it metal? A pipe? Miriam shuddered, crouched over the object. It was the tea pitcher, its rim veined with cracks. Shreds of mist wafted overhead and Miriam yelled Evelyn's name. She closed her eyes, an ear turned to the sky. Listening became physical, her shoulders flexed, her neck stiff.

Miriam heard nothing but the wind, and then it struck, churning tumults of rain, and she hugged her knees, chin to her chest to shield her face. Trembling in the bubbling mud, Miriam felt her mind sliding. She willed her imagination toward the way her mother used to sing Sunday school songs while she gardened, the way she'd wrinkle her nose when working her puzzles.

But Miriam's will faltered, and she bolted from her stance and flailed into the corn behind her, swimming through the rows. She cried as she had that evening when, outside Freely's Diner, boys in school jackets taunted Evelyn from the bed of a pickup, yelling filthy things, whistling, with everyone around, Walt Freely and Pastor

Hamby, Doc Peterson and half the church, as they'd all just come from her mother's funeral. But no one rebuked the boys. They all just shied away to their cars, and Miriam couldn't tolerate such a disgrace, and shouted down the boys, a terrible scene of cursing, wailing, of men ushering her away.

Evelyn drove them home. Miriam didn't want to go back into her mother's house and walked down into the field, the corn to her knees, wishing, even then, it was high enough to hide her from the world, and the world from her.

Miriam stepped from the corn and out into a corridor like all the others. The clouds had cleared. In the sky hung a crisp white moon. Nubs of stalks glistened, as did puddles pocking the field. Many puddles were impressions of boots, and Miriam followed them.

Soon the corridor dipped into a swale of standing water. Miriam paused before going down. She gazed into the water, struck by a flash of recognition. She'd stood here before. Stood in this very spot, squinting down into darkness. Suddenly she felt it, a memory in her muscles, the weight of a pipe, the cracking jolt up her arm.

She rushed down into water to her shins, to her thighs. Bracingly cold, she thrashed, grasping through the muck to find what she knew was there. But it was only water, only mud. Miriam crawled out wheezing. She sat slumped, her boots still in the pool. Boot prints covered this rise, frantic prints gouged in the mud.

Miriam sensed someone behind her. She turned and through a blur of tears saw a yellow shirt at the top of the slope, a bow poised, an arrow aimed down at her.

The arrow passed as a hiss, a bee sting to her ear. The boy gaped down, the bow now at his side. He turned, ran. Miriam pressed a hand to her ear. Blood came off on her fingers.

She moved without thought, rising, following the prints in the mud. Where they ended, the boy's legs stretched out from the rows. He sat upright, his bow clutched to his chest, his eyes craters of rust, lidded, vacant.

Miriam knelt beside him. His skin was cold, his thin body quaking. Her parka was wet, but dry inside, and she wrapped it around his shoulders. He leaned stiffly against her. She pulled him to her, then laid them back in the corrugate.

Corn tassels glittered above them, framing the night sky. The boy began to moan, his teeth pressed to her throat, his cries far more than sounds, as if some violent brood were clawing to escape him.

Miriam steeled her grip on the child and studied the stars in their multitudes. Points of light slowly took form, the black matter of space a shoreless lake of stars, a latitude of boundless depth, and she strained her eyes, trying to see beyond her vision's means, trying to glimpse the flesh of an upturned palm.

4

Dawn rose hot. The ground steamed. In Miriam's yard, the sheriff made calls to mobilize volunteers. Evelyn cleaned and bandaged Miriam's ear, as she sat on her porch under a blanket. Miriam said nothing about the boy shooting the arrow, and now watched him and his father out in the drive. The McGahees stood separate from everyone, spoke to no one, not even each other.

Pastor Hamby arrived by eight thirty. Miriam watched him talk with Helen, who'd met him at his car. He shook hands with Seamus. Miriam saw Seamus nod, and then Pastor Hamby spoke to the boy, who stared at the gravel and didn't move.

By nine, twenty men from the volunteer fire department mingled in the yard. By nine fifteen, K-9 units from Fairmont pulled into the drive. Evelyn made muffins, offered them around. Helen came onto the porch and told Miriam to stay put, assuring her they had plenty of help and would find the boy.

Then Seamus McGahee was there at the bottom of the steps, his eyes glaring sullenly up at her. The boy stood at his hip, his hair still flattened with mud, still wearing her parka. Helen turned to them, as well, and they were all quiet.

"Warned them boys to stay out your field," Seamus said, in an awkward explosion of words, glancing sideways at his son.

They watched the child, waiting. Then Seamus smacked the boy's head, and the boy blurted, "Sorry, ma'am."

Miriam stared at the child, at his ugly expression.

The boy took off the parka and dropped it on the porch steps. His yellow T-shirt, now ripped across the neck, clung to his thin frame.

Then the McGahees turned and stalked back up the driveway and toward their truck. Once they climbed inside, the sheriff peered down at Miriam.

"Anything I ought to know here?"

The volunteers had begun down the hill, stumping toward the field. Miriam watched McGahee's truck rumble slowly away, and shook her head.

Members of Miriam's church arrived, hauling food and water out to the volunteers. Searchers scoured the stream bank, peered into every shadowed corner of Miriam's barn. Helen asked Miriam to search her own house, and she and Evelyn crept about like the undead, opening closets, moving boxes, shining a flashlight into the attic, into the narrow slot behind the boiler.

All the while, seventy police, with eight dogs, and fifty firemen methodically paced the corn without ceasing, dozens of civilians flanking the field's edges in case the boy emerged unnoticed. The mud made things terrible, Miriam overheard a red-bearded fireman tell Helen. Hard enough to keep their footing, let alone find a child. The staties brought in a helicopter, circling low, the stutter of its propellers drowning out the baying hounds, voices hollering the boy's name.

Miriam sat on her porch in a rocker, just waiting for them to find him, to see him carried out, a rag doll in some stranger's arms. But they found nothing. A little after five, Samuel Franklin trod up the hill and told Miriam they were having trouble keeping track of the rows, that the searchers were confused by the maze.

She knew what he wanted. "Cut it down."

"You sure?" Samuel said.

Miriam nodded.

He patted her shoulder.

Evelyn sat on the top porch step, her head leaned against the banister. She'd not spoken, not moved, for an hour. Now she stood and faced her mother. "I'm going to lie down," she said.

"All right, sweetie," Miriam told her.

Evelyn slunk past them, disappeared into the house, and Miriam heard her footsteps going upstairs.

"This sure is a thing," Samuel said, gazing out over the valley, the yard a scuttle of commotion.

"He's in there," Miriam said.

By seven dusk had passed, the air hardening to a chill. The crews sulked back to their trucks. Miriam watched them from the parlor window. The house lay dark, but she hadn't the will to switch on the lights. Then they were all gone, even the pastor and sheriff sliding off without bidding good night. Miriam didn't mind. They must all feel it, too. Everyone exhausted. Everyone just a little bit lost.

She found Evelyn sitting on her bed in a nearly dark room, a suitcase opened at her feet, underclothes and shirts neatly packed.

"Evelyn?" Miriam said, softly, from the doorway.

Evelyn's shoulders lifted and fell.

The night was clouded. Scant light trickled in through the windows. A clock's red numbers glowed on a nightstand. Miriam stepped in beside her daughter's bed. They'd never bothered to change Evelyn's comforter from when she was a girl, still a pink and purple quilt with little balls of yarn fringing its edges.

"I had a terrible dream," Evelyn said.

Miriam picked up a stuffed animal, a tattered elephant they called Mr. Gray.

"About that boy," she added. "About them finding him in the trunk of my car."

Miriam tapped Mr. Gray's floppy ear.

"I have to get away, Mama," Evelyn said. "Going to go get set up again for school."

"All right."

Evelyn leaned over and Miriam heard the suitcase being zipped.

"You could go tomorrow. I'll make you breakfast."

Evelyn's shoulders fell slack, her chin to her shoulder. "Can't sleep here anymore." Her voice quavered. "Got to go. I've got to."

"Wish I could, too."

Evelyn wiped her eyes, raised herself up. "I'll be all right. Don't worry. I'll be fine."

Miriam lowered herself onto the bed. So many nights she'd sat here, reading stories, singing songs to her daughter before tucking her in. She grabbed Evelyn's shoulders, trying to embrace her. At first, Evelyn held rigid, but then she turned toward her mother and Miriam felt her daughter become flesh.

They clutched each other, the heat of Evelyn's breath warming Miriam's neck. Miriam wanted them to lie on the bed and not ever get up again. But then Evelyn let go, and Miriam did, too.

Evelyn grabbed her suitcase and left the room. Miriam stayed on the bed, listening, as Evelyn clipped downstairs. Soon the kitchen cupboards squeaked, cans clanked in the pantry, and then, at last, the front door opened and closed.

Only then did Miriam rise. She lagged downstairs to the parlor window and looked out over the drive. Evelyn loaded her suitcase in the backseat of her car, loaded another sack into the passenger seat. Then her daughter was but a shadow behind the wheel, the headlights brightening the old Ford and a swath of trampled yard.

The little car paused at the end of the drive, its brake lights holding, and Miriam imagined Evelyn having second thoughts before the car finally turned onto Old Saints Highway. Then the car was gone and no lights shone anywhere Miriam could see.

With the first glint of dawn, Miriam rose from her chair in the parlor. She'd not slept, her tiredness an atrophy to her body. She shuffled into the kitchen, struggled to lift the coffee down from the cupboard. She made an oven's worth of biscuits and scrambled two dozen eggs, fried an entire slab of bacon. She changed from her slippers into her sneakers, pulled her hair into a ponytail.

Then they were there, a truck horn honking, voices calling outside. From a window in Evelyn's room, Miriam watched them unload tools from a truck, the morning hazed and damp. Men clapped each other on the back, some smiling, laughing. They sipped from thermos cups, the hoods of their sweatshirts drawn over their heads. If she hadn't known what they were preparing for, she might think they were building a barn or digging an irrigation trench, just any workday between weekends.

The food sat in the kitchen, on trays covered in foil. She'd planned to set up a table on the porch. But now, facing them seemed unimaginable, like a ghost greeting the living. Miriam would've sent Evelyn out in her place, if her daughter was here.

Miriam turned to Evelyn's bed, smoothed out wrinkles in the

comforter. She told herself she couldn't lie down, that she had to go out among those in the yard. But then she was clearing away stuffed animals and stretching herself out on the bed.

By the bedside clock, Miriam saw it was noon. All morning she'd been numbed by the drone of machinery, the buzz of saws, and now forced herself to sit up, to lift her feet and drop them to the floor.

She peeked out the window, careful to not be seen from below. Nearly a third of the field had been cleared, a harvester parked out there, men toting corn knives and chain saws, others gathering felled stalks and heaping them in great mounds. A fire burned midfield. A black gout of smoke split the sky, the clouds sagging tedious like things soon to fall.

Miriam was a husk, nothing but flesh and thought. She grabbed a pillow from the bed and lay on the floor, on a little shag rug. Beneath Evelyn's bed, there in the cramped darkness and clumped in dust, the unblinking eyes of a toy elephant peered out at her.

She heard knocks on the front door, heard him enter the foyer, calling her name, heard him taking the stairs. Then Pastor Hamby was in the room and helping Miriam off the floor to sit on the bed. She said she was sorry, trying to explain she hadn't been sleeping much at night.

The pastor just sat holding her. "I get you something?" he finally asked.

"I'll be all right," Miriam said. "I'll get up and get moving now."

"Evelyn around?"

Miriam shook her head. "She went to the city, back to school."

"I'm sorry."

"Should've gone back a month ago." Then Miriam stood and brushed at her clothes.

He stood, too, more than a head taller than she. "Birdie?"

"Yeah?"

"You're not alone."

She pushed a strand of hair behind her ear, stepped past him and toward the doorway. "Sometimes you are."

"That's not true. Not ever."

Miriam wanted to be alone, wanted him gone. She wanted to lie back down on the rug and go back to sleep. But she knew he wouldn't allow it. She walked out of Evelyn's room and forged downstairs as if she'd found new purpose, though once in the parlor she didn't know what to do with herself.

She saw them in the yard, all the searchers, the news van parked out on the shoulder of the road. She turned away from the window, passed the pastor once more, and ducked into the foyer, figuring this as the only place there weren't any windows. She plopped onto the stairs. Pastor Hamby leaned against the banister, staring off at the door.

"They find him?" Miriam asked.

He shook his head.

Miriam rubbed her knees. "Don't know what to do. How to act with all this."

The pastor stood upright, his hands in his pockets.

They regarded each other in silence, Miriam staring up into his big solemn face. Then she glanced off into the parlor and became aware of the fading light, of how late it must be.

"I'm going to take a shower," she declared.

"Should I stay?"

"I can wash my own back."

The pastor didn't laugh, or even grin, but simply moved toward the door. His hand on the doorknob, he turned. "Promise we'll have that breakfast soon."

Miriam nodded, crossed a finger over her heart.

Miriam showered until the hot water turned cold. She slid into her robe, wiped steam from the mirror. She'd never liked her face, not even when her skin was young. Something in its angles made her harsh. She believed people avoided her because of her face, even Evelyn's father, whom maybe she'd once loved but hardly thought of anymore.

Then Miriam considered her own father, who was killed in a war, somewhere in Cambodia, when she was a toddler. She clearly recalled her mother weeping in the parlor, church ladies in gloves and hats stroking her arms, another lady bracing Miriam on her lap and whispering *there, there, darling*.

Miriam sat back on the hamper, trying to recall her father's face. She closed her eyes, searching her mind, but couldn't see him at all, not a single image that wasn't from a photo, and this seemed terribly sad to her, though she didn't feel sad.

Studying her legs, the blue veins webbing her shins, Miriam felt eyes set upon her. She glanced up quickly, as if a face would hover there, but saw only a light fixture damp with steam, the silhouettes of bugs gathered in the bowl of its globe.

The field was shorn, the yard empty. The search had gone elsewhere. Miriam considered calling Helen, or Pastor Hamby, for an update. In an impulse of bravery, she decided to drive into town. But she balked on the porch, staring out at her mother's old truck, then found herself tromping down the hill.

The field was bowed like the back of beast. She stepped over nubs, trudged through the mud. Soon the ground rose and became firm. Like in a dream, she glimpsed objects on the land, found herself in what had been the rotunda. The table was tilted but standing, the chairs pushed in. A white candle stood perfectly erect in the mud, as if atop a child's cake.

Miriam glanced back at her house perched atop the hill. How remarkably close it seemed without the corn. An engine downshifted out on the road. From a distance Miriam noticed a white truck trolling by, slowing. Someone in the passenger side rolled down the window to get a better view. Miriam didn't recognize who it was, but raised her hand, and the truck sped off.

It took her most of the day, but she found it. On the slope of a swale, half buried, she lifted a length of pipe, grooved at one end, a welded joint at the other. She inspected it closely, tried to wipe it clean, the mud smearing over its cold dull metal.

Back in the kitchen, she ran hot water in the sink. She used dish detergent, the water steaming, almost too hot for her skin to bear. She scoured the pipe with a pad of steel wool.

Then she took the pipe into the pantry, studied the pantry's full shelves. Miriam decided upon a spot, slid the pipe behind large tins marked SUGAR and FLOUR. She rearranged the tins, shifting them one way, then back over again, eyeing it from every angle until the pipe was thoroughly hidden.

5

From the kitchen table, Miriam heard a rapping on the front door. It would not stop. She hurried into the foyer, opened the door to a child she barely recognized as the elder McGahee, his eye swollen shut, nose crooked, mouth and chin and throat coated with blood, the neck of his yellow shirt stained brown with it. His feet shifted as might a drunk's, one arm hung as if it had no bones. His seeing eye pleading, Miriam peered beyond him, scanned the empty drive and yard and field, then helped him inside.

She sat him on the couch, dabbed at the blood with a warm washcloth. The boy did not flinch, didn't seem to feel at all.

"Who did this?" Miriam asked, in a whisper.

The boy's lips, shredded and swollen, parted, though no words came out.

"Was it your daddy?"

The boy struggled to swallow, then, ever so slightly, nodded.

Sheriff Farraley arrived within the hour. She examined the boy, her face twisted in disdain. "Gracious," she growled, inspecting the bruises down his arm. Gently, she lifted the boy's shirt, cringed at the sight. Angry welts, raised and infected, cut the child's back. Miriam saw the welts, too, and suddenly she felt nauseous, found herself backing away.

"Where's Evelyn?" the sheriff asked Miriam.

"Evelyn?"

"She's a nurse, ain't she?"

Miriam tried to still herself, tried to not let it show on her face. "She's gone to the city. For school."

Helen eased down the boy's shirt. "Your daddy done all this?"

A whimper escaped from the child. Tears welled in his open eye. He seemed to be staring at Miriam, muttered something she couldn't comprehend. Then he tried again, clearly saying from one side of his mouth, "Yes, ma'am."

Veins popped at the sheriff's temples. "It's all right now," she soothed. "Ain't nobody going to harm you no more."

They wrapped him in a blanket and laid him in the back of the squad car. The sheriff told Miriam she'd take him to town, would have the pastor and his wife take the boy to the hospital, look after him for the night. Then she'd go see about Seamus McGahee.

Miriam watched them leave, then returned to the kitchen. It reeked of spoil, and there to her dismay sat the trays of breakfast she'd made two days prior. She grabbed a trash bag and dumped the food, trays and all. All around, the house lay in shambles. What they must've thought, Miriam considered, the place stinking, mud across the floors.

She filled a bucket with steaming water, added pine cleaner, and began to mop the kitchen tiles, then the hall to the foyer. By the pantry she paused. She leaned her mop against the wall, stared at the pantry's closed door.

Miriam whirled back into the kitchen, treading over what she'd just mopped. She found her purse on the counter, her phone inside. She dialed Evelyn's cell number. She listened to the ticking of its ring, and then Evelyn's voice saying she couldn't come to the phone. Miriam hung up. She dialed again with the same result. Then again.

Miriam returned to the hall and took up the mop and continued to clean, the loop ends trailing muddied water, her eyes set fast to the boot tracks smeared across the floor.

Miriam stared at the truck's door. She'd barely slept, was starving. Like a child gathering her nerve to leap into a quarry pond, she shut enough of herself down to grab the handle. Quickly, she opened the door, climbed inside. For months the truck had sat dormant. The engine coughed, then sparked with a roaring shudder.

The sky hung overcast, the roads damp. She passed the McGahee house, dark and still like something abandoned, then veered onto the road to town. She found the pastor in his office, and soon they sat across from each other in a booth in Freely's Diner.

They gabbed about the change in the weather, about deer season approaching and the price of grain. The pastor ordered chicken-fried steak, said nothing about the McGahee boys, not the missing one, not the one at his house.

Others came in, Tom Duffy and Merle Hamden stopping at the

end of their table. The pastor teased them about their weight, and Merle stood sideways and asked Miriam if he'd win a prize at the fair. Then Samuel Franklin was there, too. He sat beside Miriam, telling about a man from Mountford who was teaching his son to drive stick, and accidentally lurched his John Deere into a cow pond. When he left, Samuel squeezed the ball of Miriam's knee, gave her a wink.

They finished their breakfasts. Tin signs hung above Pastor Hamby's head, rusted signs for ginger ale and cigarettes.

He tore the corner of his napkin. "How's Evelyn?"

"She's tough," Miriam said.

He sighed, his face slackening. "I worry about her. This town's full of old people. No place for a young person with half a brain." He sipped his coffee, eyeing her over the rim. "Got something tricky to ask you, Miriam."

A chill spread through her.

He set down his coffee. "Mavis Delforth's running a clothing drive for that church in Hollins Bay, asked if we could rustle up some donations." With heavy eyes, Pastor Hamby explained he thought Miriam might gather up her mother's clothes, how it might help her put some things to rest, help her get on with living.

Miriam was troubled by the relief she felt, but nodded.

The pastor set a huge hand over hers. With a solemn tone, he added, "Your mama always dressed so nice for a country woman."

Miriam went straight to her mother's closets. She cried as she worked, carefully folding dresses, stacking pants and blouses, loading them neatly into boxes, then sealing them with packing tape.

Things vanished. People vanished. Clouds gave way to sun gave way to night. Only feelings, like spirits, endured, branded to the back of our eyes, laced into our marrow. Miriam lifted a sweater to her face, blue and soft and threadbare at the elbows, still holding a hint of her mother's scent. Try as she might, she couldn't imagine her mother on streets of gold, washed in ethereal light, couldn't even imagine her mother wearing this sweater, which had been her favorite.

Miriam could only recall her mother as she'd seen her that day at the morgue, a sheet to her chin, her eyes sewn closed, another sheet to cover the hole in her skull. She considered this life and the next, decided Heaven and Hell were just where the living chose to put you once you passed, then eased her arms into her mother's sweater and lifted a box to carry downstairs.

The next morning, Miriam drove into town, her truck packed with boxes to be delivered to Pastor Hamby. But then she passed the church and cemetery, turned onto Gunderson Road. A mile later, she drifted onto the on-ramp for the interstate.

Traffic was light as she sped through vast flats of farmland. After twenty minutes, the auto plant and its stacks emerged. She passed an enormous cathedral with its acres of parking, and then came the homes, countless homes of similar design, and more cars, driving fast but tight, and Miriam took the ramp marked for the city center.

A billboard for the college loomed from an overpass, a young woman gleefully hurling a graduation cap into the air. Miriam saw signs, arrows, for the college, and passed them all. Stoplight after stoplight, she considered turning back. But then she was there, the courthouse an enormous brick building taking up much of the block.

Miriam passed through the metal detector. A portly woman with bright orange hair waved a wand down her front, glanced at her license. She followed the throng to a signboard listing cases and courtrooms in red lights. She found the case: STATE V. FARNER, 3A.

Miriam rode a crowded elevator to the third floor. It let off onto a landing, camera crews setting up, a blond-haired woman holding a microphone, a black man taping cables to the floor. Miriam wove through them all, found room 3A.

She entered with all the others, entered like anybody. The back half of the courtroom consisted of long benches. It felt like church, and Miriam took a seat on the aisle and near the door. People politely shuffled in past her, and soon the benches were packed and folks crowded the back and along the sides.

Miriam wondered who they were, all these people in their private lives who woke and dressed and drove here, and passed through the security to see a trial. She didn't recognize a single face. For a moment, she felt this must be the wrong room. But then, at one of two tables facing the judge's bench, Miriam noted an attorney she'd met once, months ago, a frumpy woman hunched and shuffling papers.

The air hung stagnant. Miriam's eyes ached. She hadn't eaten breakfast. Her stomach panged, and she pushed up her sleeves and fanned herself with her wallet.

A door at the side of the room opened, and the crowd turned at once. Miriam craned her neck. In shuffled a young man in pressed jeans and a plain gray sweater, the sweater loose over his frame, his hands gathered at his crotch, wrists cuffed. One officer walked ahead of him, one behind, and they led him to the far table, where he sat beside a balding man in a wrinkled suit.

Miriam didn't know much about him. She heard his sister and mother lived out in Haney, heard they had to move after what happened. Clean-shaven, his hair parted at the side, he looked a bit like the young man who played organ at the church. Looked like the boy who'd load your hay or change your oil. Looked like anybody you might think you know.

She'd imagined this moment so many times, how she'd feel seeing him, the pain, the hatred. Watching him now, she felt only a hollow sadness. The bald lawyer whispering in his ear, Miriam realized she'd learn how he became what he was that day, and judgment would be passed. Then she became horrified, as if she, too, were on trial, and like a mirror thrust before her Miriam recognized her own face was unwashed, her hair barely combed. She reeked of pine cleaner and wore the jeans and old sweatshirt she'd worn for days.

Savage heat flushed her face. Her ears buzzed. Miriam rose and spun into the aisle. An officer by the door, a silver-haired man with a misshapen lip, held up a palm.

"Judge's coming," he lisped. "Go out, you can't come back."

Evelyn's apartment was the attic of an old gabled house, the only house on a street lined with larger, newer buildings. The house had once been grand, but now sat shabby, nests in its gutters, shingles missing across its roof. Miriam climbed the fire escape, knocked on Evelyn's door. Waited, knocked again. The apartment's windows hung out over nothing, too far from the stairs to peek through.

Miriam returned downstairs and walked around to the grand stone porch and rang the bell. Lights inside shone through the door's frosted glass. Miriam heard someone shuffling with the locks, a woman's voice asking her to be patient.

The door opened and there stood Mrs. Jamison, who owned the house, frail and stooped, her ashen skin crinkled like wet paper.

"Mrs. Jamison," she said. "It's Miriam Swenson. Evelyn's mother." The old woman dressed in a skirt and a heavy wool sweater, wore patent-leather shoes. Miriam tugged the hem of her sweatshirt, as the woman's eyes grazed her up and down.

Mrs. Jamison grinned, her dentures stained the color of tea. "Yes, yes," she said. "Come in, dear."

Miriam stepped inside, but didn't move from the doorway. "I've come to see my daughter." She pointed upward. "Don't have a key. Was hoping you'd let me in."

Mrs. Jamison waved a hand. "Sure, sure," she said, turning. "Let me get the keys." She toddled off toward the back. The house lay quiet but for the ticking of a tall wooden clock. Pale blue carpets covered the polished floors. It reminded Miriam of a dollhouse, with its delicateness and shadows.

The old woman called for Miriam. Miriam crossed into a room with a long oval table and newspapers stacked head high all along one wall. The woman struggled carrying a paper grocery sack. Miriam took the sack from her. It was filled with mail, envelopes and catalogs, a little package set on top.

"Didn't know what to keep or throw away," Mrs. Jamison said. "Not that that's for me to decide."

Miriam stared into the sack.

"Kept it all since Evelyn went home."

Miriam, a bit confused, nodded. "Thank you."

"Good, good," Mrs. Jamison chirped. She retrieved a ring of keys from her sweater's pocket. "She's coming back soon, then?"

A deluge of thoughts flooded Miriam's mind. "She's going back to school," she said, at last, watching the woman's narrow lips.

"Oh, wonderful," Mrs. Jamison gushed. "It'll be so nice to see her. I've missed our little chats. She's a wonderful old soul, that Evelyn."

Mrs. Jamison let Miriam into the apartment. Alone, she roamed the attic, one long room of brick walls and exposed beams. A bottle of diet soda, filmed with dust, sat out on the counter. In the refrigerator she found a sack of moldy carrots, a brown head of lettuce, a rancid tub of cottage cheese. When she turned on the kitchen tap, rust-water spat until the stream ran clear.

At the far end of the room sat the bed, its covers undisturbed.

Miriam sat on the bed and dumped the sack of mail. Just bills, junk mail. Miriam held the wrapped package, decided to open it. Inside was a box of checks in Evelyn's name, vanity checks depicting the planets in their orbits around the sun.

Outside a tall window stood a giant locust tree, its wet branches black, its leaves shimmering gold against the gray. Miriam watched the boughs sway and called Evelyn's cell phone, listened to her daughter's voice-mail message, cherishing each spoken word until the beep and the white silence.

Miriam woke on Evelyn's bed, the tree outside etched into the night. She left without locking the door behind her, drove the near-empty city streets, passed semis on the highway, the slipstream pulling her toward the centerline. Coming into town, the half-light of dawn bled over the rolling hills. As Miriam pulled into her drive, the risen sun spilled a silvery sheen over her bald field.

Miriam crossed the wet yard. Up on the porch, two dogs stirred, knocking into her legs, wagging their tails. Their coats were caked in mud, cockleburs matted into Wooly's tail. Miriam crouched and petted them. They licked her face, trembling, their skins loose.

She knew they must've been on their own, must be famished. The dogs followed her into the house, whining as she hurried into the pantry. She found cans of beef hash on a high shelf. Then she glanced at the sugar, the flour.

The dogs sniffing about her feet, Miriam regarded the tins. She slid aside the flour first. Then the sugar. She took down the pipe and felt its weight in her hand. Light-headed, she passed into the kitchen and set the pipe on the counter and opened the hash and poured the meat into bowls for the dogs. The dogs ate greedily, bumping their bowls as they lapped up the meat.

Miriam watched them awhile, then grabbed the pipe and left

again into the hall. She'd not even taken off her jacket, the truck keys still in her pocket, and though her mind was a mess and she was not sure she was fit to drive, her body moved, as if without her, toward the door.

6

Miriam sat parked in front of Freely's General, the bottom floor of a three-story brownstone, staring at the length of pipe laid across her lap. A knock came on the passenger window. There stood Walt Freely, in a red nylon jacket and feed cap. He motioned for Miriam to roll down the window and she did.

"Hello, darlin'," Mr. Freely said, and from under one arm he lifted a pumpkin and reached through the window to set it on the truck's seat. "On the house," he said, then slapped the truck door.

The pumpkin was bright orange, almost perfectly round. A white scar marred its flesh near the stem. Miriam laid the pipe on the seat beside it, then opened the door and climbed down from the truck.

Light from the store shone onto the walkway. In the front window hung butcher-paper sale signs, and smaller signs, an artist's rendering of the missing boy. She stood pretending to study the sale signs in the window, stealing glances at the boy's picture. The artist's rendering didn't look a bit like him.

She meandered to the end of the building, then turned down the alley. A set of wooden steps led to the second and third floors, the third floor where Helen Farraley lived, the second being the sheriff's office. The office door was locked, and through the glass Miriam saw it was dark inside. She glanced up to Helen's apartment, light shining warm from its windows.

Miriam was about to start up the stairs, when a shadow moved in the office. She tapped the glass, and moments later Helen was opening the door. Miriam and Helen nodded to each other, and Miriam stepped into the room, which had a desk, a coatrack, a treadmill, a metal door at the back that was the jail.

Helen's face was slicked with sweat, her hair mussed. She was dressed in a tracksuit, a towel around her neck. "Was just working to get my old pants to fit," she said, and took her officer's hat from the coatrack and placed it gently onto her head. "You hanging in there?"

Miriam stared at the hat as if to see into Helen's thoughts. "Was shopping," she said. "Thought I'd come see you."

"What a nice surprise."

"Was wondering what happened. With the boy, I mean."

"You haven't heard?"

"No."

The sheriff chuckled. "Our grapevine needs watering." She stood quiet a moment, then walked behind her desk. "You want coffee?" she asked. "I'll put a pot on if you want?"

"I'm fine."

Helen sat at her desk. She blotted sweat from her chin, tossed the towel on the floor behind her. "No regard for humanity," she said. "None whatsoever." She looked up at Miriam. "You know him well?"

"The boy?"

"The father."

Miriam thought a moment. "No."

Helen motioned to a chair across the desk from her, and Miriam sat. "Talked to his kin yesterday," Helen said. "His cousin lives out by the Prospect Dairy. Says McGahee used to live down by Petersburg. Says he moved here to get away from things, that his wife died giving birth to that youngest one. Says he might of been all right if she'd of lived." The sheriff leaned over her desk, rubbed her knuckles against her chin. "Don't know how much I believe it, a man like that." She dug a piece of paper from the mess on her desk. It was the same picture that hung in the store window. "Didn't have a single photo of the boy." She studied the picture. "What kind of man doesn't have a picture of his own boy?" She set the paper back onto the pile. "Though I guess it all makes sense, really."

Miriam didn't understand, but stayed quiet.

"Anyway, we went to ask about what happened with that older boy. Was smart enough to bring Harvey and Sid Bandy along. But then I forgot who it was, just went in like I was going to chat over tea." She chuckled sadly. "Ol' Seamus come at me with a kitchen chair." Then the sheriff took her hat off, winced, set the hat onto the desk. "Miriam?"

"Yeah?"

"I always liked your mama," she said. "I'm sorry I didn't say it sooner. It just never seemed a good time to get it said, like if I liked your mama it might hurt you more somehow. But I did. You always knew where you stood with her."

"Not always," Miriam heard herself say.

Helen rubbed a hand over her hair. *"Not always,"* she repeated. "Ain't that the truth of the world?"

Miriam regretted saying it. "Thank you, Helen."

The sheriff sat still, her head lowered. "I've just been thinking about her a lot this week. About how you got to know people." She looked up, peered deep into Miriam. "That's my job, really. To know people. I realized this and now it's got me all screwed up. Because it ain't how they train you. All that innocent until guilty bullshit. 'Cause out here, some are guilty the moment you lay eyes on 'em, and what the law ought to do is to stop 'em 'fore they can do what they're born to do. What the hell good am I otherwise? Serve and protect?" Her eyes peeled across the office. "I'm nothing but a broom.

Someone calls in a mess and I go sweep it up." Helen straightened herself, pushed at some papers on her desk. "I'm sorry, Miriam," she said. "I shouldn't go on like that. It's been a hard week."

"You're so strong," Miriam said.

"I'm a broom. A damn broken broom."

Then Miriam wanted to confess everything, wanted to get it all out and be done with it. But the words stuck high in her throat, like a bone gone sideways.

"He going to stay in jail?" she mumbled.

"McGahee?"

Miriam nodded.

The sheriff's jaw flexed. "He'll die there if I get my way."

Miriam licked her lips, her mouth suddenly dry. "You think he killed that boy?"

Helen scooted to the edge of the seat. "Can't see the wind, but you don't have to think to figure what's blowed off your hat." Then she rose and walked to the window that overlooked the strip. "Had a hundred folks to look for a boy that might be alive. Made some calls the other night, seeing who might help look over that McGahee lot, and suddenly everyone's busy. Not a minute to spare."

A heaviness, like hands on her shoulders, pressed upon Miriam, and she had to push herself up to rise from her chair. Outside, the rain fell in fits. She stood behind the sheriff and watched the sky swirl above the rooftops. "What about the older boy?"

The rain hissed as static. Helen turned to Miriam, and through the gloom offered something just short of a smile. "He's in the state's hands now. Ask me, the boy hit the jackpot just to get out with a soul still in him."

Miriam sat in her truck, the wipers shushing, the side windows fogged. The rain had dwindled, but the sky still churned. Her headlights shone onto the McGahees' house, blankets covering its windows, yellow tape guarding the door. She felt oddly at ease, considering perhaps the others were right, that maybe somewhere in the bowels of that house, or buried in those weedy fields, they'd find a child.

She opened her door, stepped down into the dampness. She hadn't planned it this way, didn't think at all. She just chucked the pipe as far as she could, watched it thud beside the house, out in the open where anyone would find it.

Then Miriam climbed back behind the wheel and closed the door. The truck was warm. She set her palm against the side window, left a print in the hazed glass, clear but for a moment before it again began to fog.

Miriam unloaded the groceries she'd bought in town. She set the dogs' dishes in the corner of the kitchen, let the dogs eat. Then, one at a time, she carried each to the upstairs bathtub. Afterward, the dogs lay shivering by the radiator in the front hall as Miriam picked up the house and loaded laundry into the washer. She changed the bed linens. Made chicken salad, baked a cake.

While in the parlor, ironing a blouse for church, Miriam heard the dogs rise in the hall, their nails scrabbling across the floors. The front door opened. Miriam moved, with great hesitance, into the foyer. There stood Evelyn, setting down her suitcase. A riot broke in Miriam's chest. She braced herself against the wall. The dogs wriggled for Evelyn to pet them, but she only looked at her mother, dark crescents sagged beneath her eyes.

"I'm hungry, Mama," she said.

Miriam led Evelyn back into the kitchen, sat her at the table. Hands shaking, she poured her daughter a glass of milk and made her a chicken salad sandwich.

Evelyn chewed, her head leaned on her fist.

Miriam busied herself at the counter, icing the cake she'd baked.

They were silent awhile, everything stilted, everything not quite real. Then the cake was done, a white cake with strawberry frosting, Evelyn's favorite. Miriam showed Evelyn and, mouth full of sandwich, she nodded.

She didn't want to ask. She had to ask. "How was the city?"

"Fine," Evelyn said.

"Get things settled?"

Evelyn nodded, vacantly.

"For school?"

She nodded.

"How's that woman? Your landlady?"

Evelyn took a bite, chewed. "Mrs. Jamison?"

"That's right. How's Mrs. Jamison?"

"Fine," Evelyn said, swallowed.

Then Evelyn held up her empty glass, and Miriam took it and walked to the refrigerator. As she opened the door and took out the carton of milk, Evelyn shouted, *"Damn it!"*

Miriam spun to see Evelyn with her face buried in her hands. Her body shuddered as she sobbed.

Miriam rushed to her side.

Then she saw the sandwich, open-faced, a thick arc of salt trailing from the chicken salad on across the tabletop to the detached bottom of the saltshaker. Miriam took the empty shaker from Evelyn's fist. She walked to the sink, wetted the sponge, waiting for the water to warm, listening to her daughter weep. Out the kitchen window, the rain fell as flurries, flakes sticking to the pane, melting.

"Where were you?" Miriam said, quietly. Evelyn fell hushed behind her. The tap was warm. Miriam squeezed the excess water from the sponge, and turned. Evelyn stared down into her plate. "Where were you at, hon?" Miriam asked again, louder.

Evelyn traced a thumb beneath her teary eyes, did not look up. "What're you talking about?"

Miriam stepped to the table and swiped the sponge over the trail of salt. "You weren't in the city," she said, brushing salt off into her palm. "Where'd you go?"

Evelyn wiped her cheeks on her sleeve. "Don't know what you mean." She pressed the heel of her hand between her eyes.

Miriam wanted to touch her daughter, to hold her and make her feel right for what she'd done. But Miriam turned away, stepped again to the sink. She rinsed the sponge, watched the water flowing, the salt swirling down the drain.

She shut off the faucet. Snow striking the window was the room's only sound. "Where'd you put him?" Miriam asked. "Where'd you put that little boy?"

Miriam listened as Evelyn heaved long sighing breaths, each slower, softer, than the last. "Does it matter where?" she whimpered.

Miriam quietly gasped. When she looked up from the sink, a face glared back from the window. Night had come early, and she gazed at her bleary reflection in the snow-streaked glass, stared at the room behind her, its faded wallpaper, its watery light, her baby girl slumped at the spot where each morning her mother had sipped her coffee and worked her puzzles.

Miriam set the sponge beside the sink, dried her trembling hands on the thighs of her jeans. Possessed by a great swelling of love, she went to her daughter and hugged her from behind, Miriam's cheek pressed into Evelyn's back. Evelyn clutched her mother's arms crossed before her, gently kissed Miriam's wrists.

Then it felt like victory, for they remained. They were still here while others were gone. Miriam pulled away from her daughter. She straightened her blouse and took up Evelyn's plate.

"Would you like some cake?"

Evelyn gave Miriam her weary eyes, and nodded.

LAZARUS

The streets were plowed and salted, filthy banks of snow climbing the poles of lit signs before strips of bright shops. The high walls of the city airport stretched for blocks, a plane lifting off, its lights fading as it passed into the clouds. A day-glo truck pulled beside Vernon, its music thumping. Stoplight after stoplight, so many cars. A line of cars smoked in a chicken restaurant's drive-through. In what looked like an old department store, a church lay between an insurance agency and a florist. Its sign by the road read:

THE KING OF ROCK AND ROLL

THE KING THAT ROLLED THE ROCK

Vernon glided through it all, feeling as he imagined young David must have as he pushed his way through lines of soldiers, sling in hand. Then he turned onto Balmoral Avenue, its row of brick buildings and blazing squares of windows, selfsame apartments flanking a road marked by streetlights and beneath them the endless line of parked cars.

One block up, he turned into the parking lot of the Avemore Condominiums. Set back from the street, the complex was a horseshoe of blond-brick buildings, seven stories high, the windows spilling light into the branches of three huge sycamores in the courtyard. Vernon found Martha's car, the old silver Cadillac that had once been his. Then he was at the end of the lot and issued back out onto the street. He trolled two more blocks before finding a break in the cars, and with great difficulty edged into the space.

His nerves buzzed. His throat was sore. He grabbed the shoe box off the floorboard and removed the lid. In the streetlight's glow, he peered down at the letters. It had to be done. He dug aspirin out of his pocket and chewed them, then placed the lid on the shoe box and opened the door.

Vernon climbed out into the cold. His breath plumed. The air stank of salt, of exhaust. He held his collar with one hand, the shoe box in the other. It was dark off by the buildings, so he stayed in the light and shuffled down the middle of the road.

Then he was at the Avemore lot, and hurried through the dark cars. He entered the snowy courtyard. Footlights marked three shoveled walkways to the building's three wings. Martha lived in the rear. Vernon took its path and entered a dimly lit vestibule with a wall of metal mailboxes. He tugged the interior door, but it was locked.

Then he saw the box of buttons marked with names and unit numbers. Vernon found HAMBY 609, pressed the button. It made no sound. He wasn't sure it was working. He waited, staring back out into the courtyard. A light rain had begun to fall, stippling the snow.

"Hello." Through the box her voice sounded far away.

"Martha?" he said, glancing about the little room, not knowing where to speak.

He stared at the box, waiting for a response. At last, the interior door buzzed and he quickly took the handle. Just inside lay the stairwell, and though he was weary from not having slept, and brittle from a three-day flu, Vernon took the steps two at a time.

Vernon pushed through a door marked 6 and leaned huffing against the wall. A door opened down the hall. In the doorway stood a man in a brown coat with a white wool collar. Vernon stood away from the wall, gathered himself. Then he saw Martha behind the man and realized the cowboy was leaving apartment 609.

The man was young, not a hint of gray in his beard. He eyed Vernon as he approached, loudly asked Martha if she was going to be all right. She patted the cowboy's arm. She wore a long sweater of white and tan cables, and hugged herself, a cup of coffee in one hand.

"You're at the right place, Vernon," she said, and Vernon realized how pathetic he must look.

"See you tomorrow," the cowboy said to Martha, then turned and extended a hand to Vernon. "I'm Vance."

Vernon firmly shook his hand. "Vernon."

"I know." The cowboy glared at him a moment, then ambled off. "Thanks for dinner," he called back to Martha. Martha waved and then her eyes fell to Vernon and the corners of her mouth sank.

Vernon followed her inside. The apartment was small and filled with furniture from the parsonage. Furniture that had been theirs, tweedy couches, the oak coffee table, the bookcase dressed with angel figurines and other country knickknacks. She'd been gone only a few months, but the apartment felt lived in. Piano music played from a stereo, their son's old boom box. Beneath a large window overlooking the courtyard, a little fountain gurgled water into a trough of slick black stones.

"Hope I didn't interrupt your date," Vernon said.

"He's a classmate." She smiled, but her tone was curt. "We have an exam tomorrow."

Vernon didn't want her to see the shoe box, and slyly set it on a wicker-seated rocker beside the door, laid his overcoat over the chair. "You going to pass?" he asked.

Martha stared hard at him. "Soon as the buzzer rang I knew who it was," she said. "I'm still in the loop, you know? Sadie Walsh says you couldn't even finish the service this morning?"

Vernon stood stiff. "He's a nice man? This Vance?"

Martha stepped close and patted Vernon's chest. "Poor Vernon," she said, teasing. "Let's get you out of that jacket and get you some coffee."

She helped Vernon out of his suit jacket, plucked off his hat, and hung them both on the doorknob. She took Vernon's arm and led him to the sofa by the window, then left off into the kitchen. He sat listening to cupboards being opened, cups clinking. A coffee cake, half eaten, sat on a small table in the kitchen, and Martha called to Vernon that he should have some.

"No, thank you," he said, though he was famished.

Martha cut him a slice and set it on the coffee table. "I'm not asking, Vernon," she said. "You look terrible. Folks've been telling me you aren't taking much care of yourself."

"Who's saying that?"

"People."

"Scuttlebutts like Sadie Walsh?"

"People who care."

Martha left again into the kitchen and Vernon eyed the cake. He slid it toward himself, but didn't pick up the fork. He watched Martha, washing up cups, pouring the coffee. He wanted to go to her, to hold her and lay his face upon her shoulder.

Martha carried in two cups of coffee and handed one to Vernon. He sipped it and it tasted wonderful, like it always had.

"It's been a long day." He drank again and closed his eyes as the coffee spread its warmth through him. Vernon sat forward, hunched over his knees.

"What's wrong, Vernon?" Martha asked.

He shook his head. "Nothing."

She laughed. "You've always been the worst liar."

"Thanks."

"Lord knows, I wish you were a better liar. But one thing about Vernon Hamby is he just can't help but let the truth be known."

Vernon nodded. "It's exhausting."

"I know it is, sweetie. Was for me, too."

"I'm sorry."

"No," she said. "I'm all done with *sorry*. No more *sorry*. Now what's wrong, Vernon?"

"Not *wrong*—" He thought a moment. "Just disappointing."

"There's no such thing as *wrong* for Vernon Hamby?"

"It's God's will."

"And you take comfort in that?"

"It's not about comfort, Martha."

She tucked her feet up under her, leaned against the armrest. "I take no comfort in it, Vernon."

"I know it. Maybe you will someday."

She grinned. "Eat your cake, Vernon. Am I going to have to feed you myself?"

"I don't want it."

"Because another man ate from it first?"

Thirty years of marriage, there was no place to hide. "I'm not here to fight, Martha."

"You need to eat," she said, firmly. "I used to not be able to get my arms around you, and now I could knock you down with a sneeze."

"I'm fine."

"You want some eggs? I'll make you an omelet?"

"Coffee's fine," Vernon said.

"I do care, you know? I don't hate you."

"Anymore."

She lowered her head. She gazed into her coffee. "Fair enough," she said, nodding. "I don't hate you *anymore*."

"I'm glad, Martha."

"In class," she said, "we've been talking about forgiveness. How no matter what you say, or how much you talk, someone isn't really forgiven until you can stand beside them without wanting to slap them in the face. Been thinking a lot about that. About a lot of things." She chewed her lip, eyes drawn inward. She looked as if she might say more, then she smiled. "Why you here, Vernon?"

Vernon glanced at the wicker rocker by the door. "Sometimes," he said, "I wake in the night and can't remember his voice, or the way he laughed."

She sipped her coffee, staring out the window at the dark sky and the lit tops of trees. "Someday maybe this'll pass, and we can just get on with our lives."

Vernon gazed again at the doorway. He shouldn't have come.

"It was Henry who called," Martha said.

Vernon's shoulders fell heavy, his chin. Henry. He took up his coffee. "Yeah?"

"He told me about the vote, about the congregation meeting next Saturday."

Vernon set his coffee back down, without having drunk. "Deacons came last night, stood around me in the kitchen with their coats on." He chuckled, sadly. "They said folks've been complaining about the music. About how I hired Dillard Hurstenberg as organist."

Martha's eyes were solemn. "Oh, Vernon. It's not about the music."

Vernon nodded. "I know it. They're cowards."

"They're your friends. It's awkward."

He pushed away the coffee cake. "I suppose."

"I'm going to the meeting Saturday night. Henry said I could stay with him and Arlene if I need a place."

"You got a home."

"I don't know about that, Vernon."

"It's as much yours as mine."

"You are kind," she said, like a lament. "You know, there's a lot of folks saying a lot of things about you. Lots of folks wanting you out as pastor." She picked at her sweater cuff. "Guess they think I want to hear it now that we're apart. But I don't. I listen and think they just don't know you. Deep down you're the kindest man I've ever met. I always believed that. Still do. I've always been so jealous of you, you know? As hard as I tried I couldn't come close to that kind of care. Nobody cares deeper than Vernon Hamby."

"That's not fair."

She tilted her head. "Maybe not."

He felt such tenderness for her. "All I ever wanted was to try and explain my mind to you."

Martha stared long at him. "There's not a corner of my mind you didn't shine a light over. Sometimes I think if only we were a little bit shallow and didn't try so hard we just might've made it."

"That what they teaching you up here in that big city college?"

"Every counselor's first client is themselves." To this, she blushed. "Oh, Vernon, there's so many damaged people. Vance was molested by his own father. His mother knew and never did a thing about it. Can you imagine such a thing? His own father? Poor guy's all alone—can't even trust himself."

Vernon's knees ached from scaling the stairs, and he stretched out his legs. "There anyone left in the world that's normal?"

"*Normal,*" Martha said. "Gosh, I hate that word."

Vernon rubbed his knees. "I'm sick of words. Sometimes," he said, and suddenly felt himself sliding into that dark place, and breathed to keep himself level. "Sometimes," he tried again, "what's needed is just a good slap in the face. Maybe if you want to slap someone you ought to. Maybe it'd help as much as anything."

Martha sat forward. "Vernon," she said, "we'd be slapping folks until our hands were raw."

"It's better than silence."

She nodded. "Yes, it's better than silence."

"I brought something," he said. His pulse surged as he stood. He walked to the rocking chair by the door and lifted off his coat. He pulled out the shoe box, held it so she could see.

Her face fell grim. "Dear Lord," she whispered. She pressed two fingers between her eyes. "He never lived away from us," she said, her voice breaking. "He went away, but his home was always with us." She stood, turned into the kitchen.

Vernon walked to stand at her back. He wanted to put his arms around her, but held himself against the urge. "It's all we have."

She turned to him. "You've never asked what I wanted. Not once. Not ever."

"Please, Martha."

Martha buried her face in his chest. Vernon embraced her, one arm tight around her shoulders, the other at his side, his hand clutching the box of letters.

They sat at the kitchen table. The letters had arrived weeks after the funeral, three letters in a large manila envelope. Martha had wanted to read them. But Vernon couldn't face them. He put the letters in a shoe box and hid them in the cellar, behind the boiler, where Martha would never look. They'd fought bitterly over the letters, said awful things they'd long kept inside. Now Vernon took them from the shoe box and laid them on the table.

"Should we read them aloud?"

"If you want," Martha said.

"Maybe we should take turns."

"Just do it, Vernon."

Vernon set aside the thickest envelope. He took up one of the others and with a butter knife sliced open the flap. Inside was a sheet of bluish paper with a scroll of vine around the edges. Vernon took a long sip of coffee. Martha sat sideways in her chair and stared out at the night through a small window above the sink.

The letter was in Wesley's neat slanting print. Vernon cleared his throat. "'Dear Mom and Pop,'" he read. "'How's everything on the green side of the world? Everything is great here aside from the war,'" Vernon read, without expression. There was a picture of a smiley face, and Vernon showed Martha. "'And the sand is killing me. Sand and more sand. I'll never go to the beach again. When I get home—'" Vernon's throat caught on the line, and he tried again. "'When I get home, I'm taking my rifle to Ed Munsen's woods and sitting in a deer stand for a month. Man I miss the woods. I'll even take the snow. It's cold here, but no snow. There was a sandstorm last week that took the paint off the trucks. No kidding. I keep fixing the same trucks. Just cleaning out sand from every tube and casing. It's been long days lately.'" Vernon held up the letter and showed Martha where Wesley had drawn a cross-eyed face with a wriggly mouth. She said nothing, turned back to the window.

"'I'd go crazy without the kids,'" Vernon read on. "'Whenever I get a break from the shop I head over to help. Me and Sergio helped paint the school last week. Kids just follow me around—got my own platoon.'" Another smiley face drawn beside this. "'I asked my sergeant if I could take off my flak jacket and helmet because I want the kids to know I trust them. But sarge said to be a good soldier and—'" Vernon had to stop. He set the letter on the table. It was what he'd feared. He pinched the bridge of his nose.

Without a word, Martha plucked the letter from the table. Her lips moved as she found her way down the page. "'But sarge said to be a good soldier and keep my brains in my head where they belong,'" she read. "'The kids call me Rocket because I raced a few and dusted them. Still got my track legs. It's a mess over here. There's more talk of us moving to BSA. Keep your fingers crossed. I miss short pants. I'll wear shorts all winter when I get home. I'll go shirtless for a year. I'll sit naked in Ed Munsen's woods. Sometimes writing these feels like I'm just writing to myself. Got the care package. Tell Ms. Peerman's class thanks for the batteries.'" Martha's voice took on a weariness. "'Tell Muggie and Sam hey—'" Martha glanced up at Vernon. Her eyes scanned the page, her lips stiff.

"What's it say?" Vernon asked.

Martha stared a moment into Vernon's eyes, then turned back to the page. She was crying now, and wiped her cheeks with a tissue. "'Send me some underwear, Ma,'" she sniffed. "'Nothing fancy. Boxers. Anything that won't hold sand.'"

Martha laid down the letter. Vernon took it up from the table, stared at the handwriting until it blurred. He grabbed the next envelope and sliced it open.

Inside was a flattened cardboard box, the packaging for a beef stew dinner—on one side a picture of a steaming bowl of stew, and on the back a short message in red marker. *Here's all I eat!!!* In large script across the bottom, *MY LEFT NUT FOR A PEACH COBBLER!* along with a doodle of a smiley face with devil horns.

"Let's hear it," Martha said.

Vernon handed it to her. He watched her turn it in her hands, watched her wet cheekbones rise. "Never serious," she said, almost proudly.

"Bet he was hoping we'd put it up on the bulletin board."

Martha grinned, dabbed at her eyes.

Vernon grabbed up the last letter. Thick, dog-eared, it sat weighty in his palm. He stared at his own name on the outside of the envelope, his address. Had the words Hamby, or Krafton, ever been written from so far away?

"Go ahead, Vernon," Martha urged.

Vernon pried up the edge with his thumbnail. He slid in a finger and tore the top. He unfolded several sheets of cream-colored construction paper. They were crayon drawings. A brown rectangular house and stick people playing soccer. A lion on its hind legs, standing atop a rock, its mouth wide and full of jagged teeth. A hooded man raising a sword beneath a huge rainbow. An egg-shaped soldier, an egg in combat fatigues, madly flapping his arms, either to fly out of, or keep from falling into, a giant smoking skillet.

Vernon held the egg-soldier picture up to Martha. She squinted, nodded. Vernon set the page on the table between them. Written on a diagonal in the corner of a page, it said: *Meet G.I. Humpty! The others are by my kids. Hard to make them smile. Pray for us!*

Then there were no more words, and the anchor whose ship was battered by a yearlong storm broke free from the reef of Vernon's heart. He felt as if he were seeping heat, as if his chest had cracked wide, then the tiles rose up and he found himself on the floor, Martha over him, pleading, *"Oh, get up, hon. Get up—"*

Her hands beneath his arms, Martha helped him stand. His legs felt numb. He couldn't see through his tears. He staggered, Martha a crutch beneath him. Then they were in a dark room and he plopped down upon a bed. She untied his shoes and took them off. His tie came loose from his neck, and Vernon lay back on the bed, rain splashing against the window and light from outside glittering across the ceiling.

Then Martha was beside him, the length of her body warm against his. She whispered into his ear for him to settle down, and he lay his cheek against hers and closed his eyes to the rain-bleary darkness.

Wind gusts rattled the windows. Vernon blinked, light from the courtyard swaying on the ceiling. He wasn't sure how long he'd slept. Martha lay in his arms, her face against his chest. Vernon carefully slid his arm from beneath her, rolled out of bed. The bed stand clock read 4:46. Every lost and wounded part of Vernon wanted to crawl back in beside Martha. Instead, he found his shoes by the door, his tie draped over a chair, and carried it all out into the hall.

The lights in the main room were still on, Wesley's letters strewn across the kitchen table. Vernon picked one of the children's drawings off the floor, the hooded swordsman beneath the rainbow. He ran his fingers along the arc of the rainbow, then set the drawing on the table and crossed to the cupboards.

He filled a glass with water. The kitchen window looked out over the lot behind the complex, an auto yard bathed in a greenish light. The wind bowed the power wires. Light posts rocked. Vernon dug aspirin from his pocket, swallowed them with the water. He retrieved his suit jacket from the front door, rolled up his tie, and stuck it in his pocket. He switched off the lights as he walked back down the hall to lean in the bedroom door.

Vernon had come here to open Wesley's letters, hoping Martha would forgive him and come back home and be his wife again. But she'd been right: even opening the letters had not been for her. Watching Martha sleep, her lips parted as if singing, and still in her clothes, in her nest of covers, Vernon felt more love for her than he'd ever felt for anything. So much of a life they'd shared, so many laughs, so many touches. But there were things people should never share, and he and Martha had those things between them, too.

He slunk back into the kitchen, studied the letters on the table. He thought of leaving Martha a note. But even if not spoken, everything had finally been said. He folded up Wesley's drawing of the egg-soldier flailing above the skillet, tucked it into his pocket.

The little fountain gurgled by the picture window. Outside, the sycamore limbs tossed and whirled. Vernon crossed the dark room, put on his hat and overcoat. When he opened the door, light slashed in from the hall, and he quickly stepped out to shut the door behind him.

The roads were slick and the one-hour drive from the city took two. At the Krafton exit, daylight flashed off the corrugated walls of the old McCallister mill. Vernon surveyed the sparkling land, playing in his mind the knobs beyond the mill, naming who lived on what road, knowing them by their fields, by their barns and kitchens and drawing rooms, knowing kids from parents, aunts from cousins, naming them each by their pains and praises. There wasn't a shadow in this town over which, at some point, he hadn't prayed.

Cattle huddled steaming by Trace Mattison's fence. Fields of winter wheat flanked the road, humped white land receding into a spread of homes, the Ollies and Nordquists, the Klangmans and two families of Borgs, smoke from their chimneys staining the blue.

Vernon slowed as he drove the long hill down into the strip of brownstones, cars parked in the ice-tracked shade between Freely's Diner and Freely's General. John Erickson's rusted Bronco. Gage Trudeau's pickup with the jib crane in the bed. Stu Bacon's old Charger with the dent in the door.

He trolled by the SuperAmerica, a plow filling at the pumps,

Mavis Strandhort in his orange cap, a cigarette in the gap of his beard, raising a hand to him. Vernon waved back. On the right, he passed the Old Fox Tavern, its lot empty but for a black Ford up on a jack and missing a tire. Then Vernon clipped over the freight tracks, the road ahead clear and straight.

He sped faster, the power wires blurring against the peerless sky. Soon came the crooked elm alone on the ridge, then the windbreak of pine, the headstones glistening in the graveyard.

Someone had plowed the drive. Vernon eased down to park at the parsonage. He stared at the big house, a light left on in the kitchen, thought of his bed inside. But the day was bright and he regarded the sunlight on the sanctuary's stained glass. He trudged across the yard to the chapel, unlocked the door, clomped up the stairs.

He loved the smell of this place, the scent of pine cleaner and old books. So much he'd miss. In the foyer hung a bulletin board covered in paper snowflakes, notices of choir programs, folks selling tack and cordwood and bluetick pups. Vernon took Wesley's drawing from his pocket, cleared a place center-square of the board, and pinned it up. Then he removed his wet shoes and pushed through the heavy doors and into the sanctuary.

Sunlight blazed through the stained glass, a mottle of colors cast over the pews. Shards of blues and purples. A glowing white dove carrying an olive branch. Greens and reds of Eden, the trees and fruit bright as jewels. A white lamb in a dark field, shepherds peering up at angels in bands of gold.

To the right were stairs. In socked feet, Vernon climbed into the balcony, a sloping box of four pews. He sat at the top and gazed out over the room. Next Saturday night all of these pews would be packed and they'd speak of him as if he were already gone and then there'd be a vote though none was needed.

Vernon suddenly felt buoyant, filled with the air of relief, the peace one feels when after much struggle and deliberation a course has, at long last, been set. The room was warm. Vernon slid gingerly down to lie in the pew, snugged his coat to his chin, and turned his hat over his eyes.

Vernon was awakened by the organ. He sat up, squinting, waiting for his eyes to take focus. Down beside the dais, Dillard Hurstenberg sat at the organ in the same green jacket, same skinny tie he wore at yesterday's service. Beneath the bass pedal's hum flourished a series of trilling notes. The music crackled, blossoming in gentle bursts. An eruption of song, whole chords rising octaves, higher, louder, Dillard's body hunched but his arms alive.

Vernon had never heard this song. The music brimmed inside him. He found himself standing. He took the balcony stairs down into the main room. The music swelled, the sound vibrating through the floor. Vernon walked the side aisle, Dillard too possessed by his playing to notice.

Vernon stood behind the boy. His mother had died a year ago. An overdose. Then, one morning, Dillard was there in the pews, staring up at the cross hung above the choir loft. Others didn't care for him, said they didn't like his playing. Vernon allowed they could argue he was wild, say he'd dropped out of school, already been twice in prison, still drank and partied and chased after girls. But no honest man could argue the boy couldn't play; Lord, he made that organ wail, his eyes shut, fingers clawing over the keys.

All at once the bombast broke to silence, a complete and breathless hush. Dillard's hands dropped into his lap. His head swung low, his back shuddering. Vernon realized he was crying. He stepped forward and set a hand upon Dillard's shoulder.

The boy flinched, startled, whirled about on the bench. "Pastor," he huffed, and his shoulders fell slack. Dillard wiped his cheeks. "Thought I was alone."

"No," Vernon said.

His red eyes batted like those of a man slapped awake. "It's all right. I mean, I'm all right."

"You sure?"

Dillard sniffled, shrugged.

Vernon sat on the organ bench beside him, could feel the boy's shoulder against his own.

"Pastor?" Dillard said.

"Yeah?"

Dillard glanced back over his shoulder, across the sanctuary, out over all of the empty pews. He hadn't shaved and a bruise on his cheek showed through his whiskers. "I just feel so bad everywhere else," he said. "But here I'm good. Here I'm all right."

Vernon slid his arm around Dillard's shoulders. He gave the boy's shoulder a squeeze, leaned into him. "What was that you were playing just now?"

"That?" Dillard said. "Oh, just letting off some steam."

"You wrote it?"

"Wrote?" he said. "Just played it, you know."

"It was beautiful," Vernon said. "It was about the most beautiful thing I've ever heard."

Dillard smirked. "You're crazy."

"Can you play it again?"

"You want to hear it again?"

"I want you to play it for everyone next Sunday. We'll have a crowd for it. I promise it'll be a crowd out the door."

"You *are* crazy."

Vernon nodded. "Maybe."

The daylight was warm on his back, and Vernon didn't want to let loose of the boy's shoulders, and Dillard didn't move.

"Pastor?"

"Yeah?"

Dillard's head was bowed, his face twisted in thought. For a time the boy was silent, and then he began to cry again. "It's 'cause of me, ain't it?" he muttered.

Vernon knew what he meant. "No."

"You leaving, though, ain't you?"

Vernon stared up at a window lit in amber, Jesus serving the fish and loaves on a Galilean hillside. "Every day's a new batch of crosses," he finally said. "All of us taking our turn." Vernon watched Dillard until the boy gave him his eyes. "Christ didn't just die for our sins, son," Vernon said. "Christ taught us how to be crucified. How to go off into the tomb. But then, after a while, that rock rolls away and the sun shines in and you get to go live some more."

Dillard touched his own lips. He wiped his eyes on his jacket sleeve. "Pastor?" he said, quiet.

"Yeah?"

"It don't have a name."

"A name?"

"The song."

"Oh."

"For the bulletin, I mean. How can I put it in the bulletin if it don't have a name?"

Vernon thought for a moment. "It's your song, son," he said. "It's not for me to name."

VOLT

The calf's black tongue hung from its muzzle, its white hide shining in the pale sunrise. Helen Farraley crouched high on the hillside, batted flies from its vacant opal eye. She'd gotten the call deep in the night, the old man's wife jabbering in ragged English. Something about something in the field. Something about killing. Helen had imagined the worst, was disgusted to find she'd been awakened over a dead calf.

"Some animal get it?" she asked Moss Strussveld. The old farmer wore a straw hat, his collar buttoned at his throat. "Some dogs maybe?"

Moss raised a shaking finger to tap his dentures. "No bite." His voice was thin and steeped in the motherland. "Animal will bite."

Helen lay a palm to the calf's throat, its meat still warm. The old man was right. No marks. "How about disease? Some illness?"

His eyes snapped to her. "My cows are well."

"Ain't it possible? The water what it was?"

"My cows are well," he said, again.

A lone cow lingered, skittishly regarding her, the rest of the herd down below the flood line, where the grassy hillside became mangy ocher dirt. Helen eyed the cow, peered out over the valley. In the far distance, the brownstones of town were scratches in the shadowed land, the sun not yet risen above the hills to wake the lows. Three months since the flood and the world still reeked of silt.

Helen stood, hooked her thumbs on her gun belt. "Listen," she said. "Got to call the vet. Not the police. Understand?"

The old man wagged his finger. "No vet," he replied. "Marta say listen, Moss. I hear. Three nights I hear. Some messing been in my cows."

Helen found herself unable to look at him. She eyed his place on the ridge, his perfect red barn and little stone house. "This ain't my job," she said. "I deal in people. People, not animals."

The old man said nothing more. He clasped his hands behind his back and hobbled uphill toward his tractor. Helen watched him struggle to climb into the seat and thought to offer a hand. But she'd worked the flood, had learned there was a limit to the help some would suffer from others.

The wind buffeted the cruiser and Helen woke with a gasp, as if sleep had dragged her under water. The tension wires thrummed overhead. The wipers rattled against the windshield. She batted her eyes, and came to focus on the quarry pond far below, the dark water riffling. Out the side window, the high grass lashed the feet of the electrical tower, its girders swaying, ever so slightly, against the weltering sky.

Thunder clapped and shook the earth and then the car was engulfed, rain thrashing the windows. By the dashboard clock, she'd slept two hours. Two hours in a blink. Two hours like nothing. Since the flood, Helen was always tired, as if the weeks of fighting water had spent years of energy.

Watching the rain assault the windows, she recalled standing beside Walt Freely in his store, the first of the flood sluicing down Elm Avenue, brown water purling over the tiled floor, over the tops of their shoes, rain pouring then no different from today.

"You fetch the animals," Freely said, his old eyes somber. "I'll set to building the ark."

The storm passed quickly. The high sun pierced the wake of sheer clouds. Helen's cell phone rang. She checked the number, saw it was Walt Freely, the town's mayor and her boss. She let it go to voice mail, then, after a minute, listened to his message. Freely sounded perturbed, asking where she was, saying the power had been knocked out in town.

Helen couldn't see a way around it and drove off the quarry road and down into the flats, the asphalt tricked and buckled, ditch banks crumbled, houses crooked on their foundations with grime-splattered clapboards painted with slogans to warn off looters. The pavement steamed. Branches strewn everywhere. A power pole leaned out over Elm Avenue, held up only by its wires.

Helen turned onto the strip. Folks congregated on the road between the three-story brownstones that housed the diner and grocery, both shops dark, the grocery store's front window gone, glass glittering on the walkway. Walt Freely, a gaunt old man in a nylon jacket that read *Freely's* across the breast, stood at her window before she could open the cruiser's door.

"Where you been?" he snapped.

Helen squinted up through the window. He'd been this way since the flood. Helen just took it all.

Freely motioned at the little crowd. "These folks pay your salary." His eyes strayed to the glass on the sidewalk, and for a moment Helen thought he might cry. Then he thumped the cruiser's roof. "Do your job," he barked, and stalked off toward his store.

Helen scanned the stolid faces. Ted Yoder and Leonard Bateman. Carol Murphy, who waited tables at the diner. A few guys from the Havesty Construction crew. None smiling, none giving her more than a glance.

Helen stayed in the car, dialed information to put her through to the power company. She worked her way through recorded messages and garbled music, was eventually told by a smoky-voiced woman the problem was a substation, the power out for most of the county. She couldn't estimate how long it'd take to get it all back up and running, couldn't say how soon they'd repair the power poles, though they'd surely start in more populated areas.

Helen called Mel Smith, a local handyman, and asked him to come right off to fix the storefront. She phoned the Pendelak twins, who were good ball players and popular in school, told them to come into town with a few classmates, saying the town was torn up again and everybody needed to pitch their part.

Sweat trickled down Helen's ribs, a line of damp marking the shelf of her stomach. She left the car and crossed the road and the walkway of broken glass to enter the grocery.

The aisle closest to the window was littered with glass and wilted magazines blown from their racks. Passing the aisles, empty of people, sparsely stocked, Helen's thoughts veered to the senior home where her mother lived, and she imagined her mother, who the day before had looked upon her like a stranger and refused to speak.

Helen found Freely at the butcher counter. The old man peered into the case, at the neat piles of chops and steaks, mounds of sausages, catfish and perch laid on garnished beds of ice.

"It's to be dark awhile," Helen told him.

Freely didn't turn. His head slowly shook, his eyes trained on the meat. "It'll go bad," he said. "It'll all go bad, won't it?"

Helen held the door for a medic wheeling a woman out to an ambulance parked under the portico. In the senior home's foyer, Helen passed a moonfaced man with long black braids inspecting an oxygen tank, a dozen or more tanks lined along the front window. In the back of the room, away from the window's heat, elderly men and women sat waiting in a row of metal chairs, each gripping an orange or red popsicle in an age-spotted hand.

The halls were dark and nearly silent. Where doors were open, sunlight cut into the hall. Helen entered her mother's room and found her mother sitting in a wheelchair. She was dressed in a pale-blue cardigan, her hands in her lap. Her face turned to Helen, but she said nothing. Helen searched her mother's eyes, which were unfocused in a way that made Helen wonder if she'd gone blind.

Helen wheeled her mother out. An exit in the back led onto a little patio overlooking a clover meadow. Higher aground, this area had been spared by the flood. Plastic pots marked the patio's four corners, pansies wet and drooping, mud trails leaking from the bottoms.

Helen held her mother's hand and more than anything wanted her mother to turn and see her, for them to talk as they once had. It'd been a year since Helen moved her to this home. A year of deterioration, her limbs weakening, her mind slipping. Helen's heart wrenched, overwhelmed by the guilt in hoping it'd all soon be over.

The door opened and out stepped Sally Winkowski, who ran the home, a woman just a few years older than Helen, her hair dyed the color of beets. In her hands she held a limp box of popsicles.

Sally pulled a popsicle from the box. "They're gonna melt," she said, offering it to Helen.

Helen took it, thanked her. "How's things?"

Sally smiled. "We're scrambling."

"Anything I can do?"

Sally patted Helen's shoulder. "We're fine." She pulled another popsicle from the box. "For Mama?"

Helen took it from Sally. She tore the paper. The popsicle was bright red and she worked her mother's fingers to hold the stick. Her mother's eyes drew onto her fist. Helen considered what it would mean to forget a life, the slate cleaned of all notions of good and bad. To be innocent again. Her mother's arm lifted and Helen watched her lick the popsicle, her eyes widening like a child's, her tongue lapping the sugar put onto her lips.

Sunlight bled through Helen's eyelids. She'd parked in the electrical tower's latticed shade, but now the sun had shifted. Helen lolled her head against the cruiser's bright window, her eyes opened to power lines bowing tower to tower then vanishing over the rim of the hill only to reappear, far below, to span the quarry pond. Sunlight dully flashed on the pond's storm-stirred water. Trucks parked down there, kids come to swim.

Her cell phone rang. She checked to see it wasn't Freely, then answered it.

"Sheriff?" It was a man's voice, soft, hoarse.

"Yes."

"Gil Henderson."

Helen straightened herself. Gil Henderson was a marshal from the county seat, an old brand type who didn't call for leisure. "How's things, Gil?"

"Busy, sister."

"That's a song I know."

"Well," he said, "afraid I'm going to have to add to it. Got to come down there. Thought I'd phone ahead."

"Appreciate it, Gil."

"It's a courtesy."

"Appreciate it," she said again.

"You know a Jorgen Delmore?"

Helen winced at the name. Her mother had taught the boy in 4-H, schooled him in taxidermy. He'd mounted a pheasant for her once, won a ribbon at the fair. Last she knew he'd enlisted in the army and was off in Iraq. "Yes, sir."

The marshal explained Delmore had been arrested in the city on felony possession, got out on bail. Said he'd missed his court date and now there was a warrant for his arrest. "Got to hunt him out," he said. "How's this look from your end?"

Helen's jaw tightened. She hadn't heard Jorgen was home, hadn't heard any of this. "Those Delmores," she said, considering how much to tell. "Well, they just ain't right."

The marshal grunted. "How well you know the boy?"

"His family's rough, but he ain't bad."

"Hell, he ain't."

"Well—"

"Got to bring him in."

Helen's cheeks flushed. "Yes, sir."

"You help us out?"

"Help?"

"Go talk with him," he said. "Smooth the road for us."

Helen tapped a knuckle against the steering wheel. "All right."

"It's a tight leash, Helen."

"That right?"

"Be there tomorrow, a.m."

"That soon?"

She heard a clicking on the line. "You help us or not, sister?"

Helen shut her eyes. "Sure, Gil," she said, rubbing her brow. "I'll do what I can."

The cabins were circled like battlements against the overgrown woods. Kids played in the middle, stomping puddles, kicking about a green plastic bottle. Some barely out of diapers, boys and girls alike shirtless and filthy. They watched Helen as she trolled the circle, searching out the address Henderson gave her. A redheaded boy, twice as tall as the rest and nothing but legs, spat on the cruiser's hood.

Helen found cabin 17. The yard was a mess, a tricycle with no front wheel, a sandbox steeped in weeds and brown water. Garbage bags covered the windows. The kids followed the car. She opened the door and told them to go home, but they didn't.

She walked a path of flat stones around to the door. She was just here to talk, tried to put on a smile, look at ease. She heard movement inside, a woman shouting.

As Helen stepped onto the stoop, a door banged at the back of the house. She heard quarreling, voices. Instinct told her to move, and she hurried around to find a bald man in jeans and no shirt, his muscled back riddled with cuts, trying to run while another man tugged his arm to keep him in the house. But the bald man tore free and dashed into the woods, the other giving chase and calling, "Jorgen, goddammit."

Helen shouted after Jorgen, too, then a shadow cast itself over her, and she spun to face a large bearded man in a red shirt. His fist struck the base of her throat. She crumpled as if her legs had lost their bones, her face hitting the ground.

Sparks hissed across Helen's vision, blood in her mouth. She tried to take her feet, couldn't catch her breath. Gasping, she bear-crawled toward the cruiser. The muddy feet of children blocked her way. She reached to push them aside, then, groaning, her lungs bucking, pulled herself up the cruiser. She opened the door, fell into the driver's seat.

Helen shut the door. Kids pressed their faces to her window, laughing. She started the motor and switched on the siren. Breathing came strained as she slipped the car into gear, rolling slowly away so as not to crush the children.

Helen gathered herself in a turnout a quarter mile down the road. Her lip was bloodied, a front tooth loose. When she inhaled, her breastbone burned. Everything that was Helen that was not her body told her to drive away, to just tell Gil Henderson she'd tried but couldn't find the boy. But her muscle and blood wanted to clutch something and not let go.

She swung the car around, drove in without slowing, the kids chasing her like dogs. She drew her pistol and strode around the cabin, avoiding the front. Mosquitoes swarmed the back door. Gun poised, she turned the knob, crept inside.

A short dark hall entered onto the main room, lit by a barebulbed lamp set on the floor. A young woman lounged on a couch. Dressed in a long black T-shirt, a silver-hoop ring in her nose, she hollered, "Gert!"

The bearded man stepped out from the kitchen, wiping his hands on a little towel. Helen trained the gun on him, screamed for him to get on the ground. The young woman shouted, cursing. The big man didn't obey. The young woman rose, arms flailing, and again Helen yelled for the man to get on the ground. He stepped hard toward her and she fired.

The man dropped to a knee, gripping his arm. He pulled his hand away and looked at it. No blood. The young woman shrieked and Helen yelled for her to shut up, then shouted at the man to lie on the ground. He did as told, his hands over his head like he'd done this before.

Helen drove a knee between his shoulders and with one hand slapped on a cuff. She holstered her pistol, wrenched his other arm and cuffed it, too. Then Helen jumped off like he was ablaze and redrew her pistol.

With one hand, she helped the man to his feet. His face was scrunched tight, drenched in sweat. The young woman shouted, "I'm calling Daddy Fay. I'm gonna."

Daddy Fay was Faylon Delmore, Jorgen's father. Helen knew it was a threat. "You shut your mouth," Helen told her, and shoved the big man out the back.

"I'll call him," the girl cried, as Helen stepped back out into the daylight and mosquitoes. "Don't you worry, Gert."

The kids were still around front, jumping up and down, the redheaded teen perched on the cruiser's hood. To Helen's surprise, the bearded man hollered, "Get off the lady's car, Casey."

The boy hopped off with a gangly dance, flipping the bird with both middle fingers. Helen opened the door to the cruiser, held the man's head so he wouldn't bump it on the roof, and ushered him down into the seat.

Helen drove the long way, south of town, to avoid the main drag. The road flanked the Big Squirrel River, its current muddy and frothing, then the new development where all the old houses had been demolished and streets of identical felt-papered frames were erected on the floodplain. Then came the old Victorians, the entire row of houses under repair, their yards planted with fresh sod and saplings.

Soon she turned into the alley behind the brownstone that was the grocery on the bottom floor, the sheriff's office on the second, her own apartment on top. She stepped out to the scent of grilled meat, and through the side alley saw people gathered in the strip.

Helen escorted Gert, who'd declared nothing beyond his right to say nothing, up into the office. The room was long and spare, the new drywall unpainted, the only two furnishings a desk and two chairs. At the back of the room was a dented metal door, the only thing salvaged from the flood. Gert balked at the jail's doorway, complained he couldn't go in when there weren't no lights. Helen told him to be a big boy and sat him on the cot, the cuffs left on, and closed the door.

Then Helen went down and around into the strip. She stayed tight to the building and slipped into the grocery. Plywood covered the storefront, and she struggled to see, had to hold a soggy magazine to the door to see a grinning hunter on its cover. Down a different aisle, she found scented candles in little glass jars. She sniffed the jars, picked one that smelled like lavender. She found matches behind the cigarette counter, then put the magazine and the candle in a plastic bag, and returned to the jail.

Gert sat where she'd left him. She lit the candle and set it on the floor, tossed the magazine at his feet. "I'll uncuff you if you behave," Helen told him. "Move wrong and I'll Mace you."

She showed him the spray, and he nodded.

Uncuffed, he stretched his arms and rubbed his wrists.

"Hungry?" Helen asked.

"Fuck yourself," he said.

She locked him in the cell, then went back down into the road. Much of the town was here, milling and gabbing. At one end of the strip was a horseshoe of grills, with Freely down there cooking burgers and steaks and chicken and fish, long tables in the street covered with buns and chips and sodas. A sign by the grills read LIGHTS-OUT SPECIAL: $5.

Helen nodded at folks she passed, afraid they'd noticed her swollen lip, worried someone would ask who she had up in the jail. Freely smiled as she approached, hollered at a teen manning a grill to pick the best steak for his sheriff. The old man wobbled over, his arms thrown wide, and though he'd never been much of a drinker Helen could smell the liquor on him.

Freely hugged her. "Sorry about earlier," he muttered.

Helen nodded, glancing up at the second-floor window, at the salt-white flood line near the roof. She asked the teen for a burger, too, and filled the plates with chips and potato salad and grabbed two sodas, the load precarious as she walked up the road.

Back in the office, she set her plate at her desk, then knocked on the jail and hollered she had food and that he should move to the back unless he wanted to get Maced. She opened the door. Gert stood at the back wall, barely visible in the candle's light. She set the burger and chips and soda on the floor, asked if he was okay. He said nothing, so again she locked the door.

Helen ate at her desk, chewing steak in the watery light from the windows overlooking the road. She knew there'd be a trial and she thought about the report she'd have to write. She'd fired her gun. It'd been an impulse, and it worried her now, not because it'd be deemed unjustified, but because she was uncertain she'd meant to miss.

Then she wasn't hungry and sat listening to the people down in the strip, Harriet Meyers singing church songs like love songs. Helen crossed to the window and gazed over the scene. Teens lounged in truck beds. Kids ran with sparklers. Men threw horseshoes in the empty lot where the SuperAmerica once stood. Others talked in the road, and though Helen had once been one of them, she was no longer sure what they said to each other, these people who saw each other day after day, week after week, until they died.

Her cell phone rang. She didn't recognize the number, thought about letting it go to voice mail, but answered at the last moment.

"Helen?" a woman's voice asked.

"This is."

"Winnie Delmore."

Jorgen's mother had been a Henderson before she married Delmore, and long ago she and Helen had been in the same class at school. "Been a while, Winnie."

"Well," she said, "seems we got a little mess here, Helen. Think we ought to get together and chat?"

"I'd surely like that, Winnie."

Helen followed Winnie's directions out into the knobs, down a snaking dirt road, and over hills bunched with sumac and sassafras. Then the road was blocked by a chain drawn taut between two trees. Helen shut down the car. For a long minute, she held her pistol in her lap. I'm just here to chat with an old friend, she thought. She set the gun inside the glove box. But then she felt all the more afraid, and retrieved the gun and snapped it back into her holster.

Helen stepped over the chain and onto a sloping dirt path. Dusky light feebly lit the canopy. The path soon opened onto a grouping of low tattered buildings. Boxes that were beehives filled the yard. A long porch fronted the house, and a portly young man in dead-leaf camos called through a window for his mother.

Helen waited in the yard, eyeing a group of men off in a corrugated shack who stared down into an aluminum crate Helen guessed was an old freezer. Then Winnie Delmore was there, drying her hands on an apron and stepping off the porch.

Helen shook Winnie's rough hand and they smiled at one another. There'd been a time they'd run in the same circles, swimming at the quarry, hunting mushrooms, drinking gin and Fanta in the

Indian caves. Winnie's face had gone fuller through the cheeks, but her blue eyes, her snaggled smile, were just as Helen remembered.

"How long's it been?" Winnie asked.

"Too long," Helen said, and meant it.

Helen followed Winnie into the porch's shade and through a screen door. The house smelled of kerosene. The electricity was off here, too, and they passed down a long dark hall into a parlor with windows facing west. The sunset leached amber light over everything. Helen sat in an armchair facing Winnie and two young women, one being the girl in black from Jorgen's cabin. Two others sat back in the shadows, ancient creatures slumped on a love seat, an afghan smoothed across their laps.

Winnie asked about friends she hadn't seen in a while, smiling, talking about the old days, how things seemed simpler back then. "That's getting old for you, though, ain't it?" she said. "Always thinking things were simpler."

She asked about Helen's mother.

"Got her over in that Quail Ridge senior home."

"You put your mama there?"

Helen peeked at the women on the love seat, skeletal and unmoving, one woman's blond wig crooked on her ashen skull. "Mama don't know where she's at. Doesn't even know me on sight." Helen forced a grin. "Part of life, I suppose."

The boy from the porch carried in a silver tray with china cups and a teapot. He set the tray on a delicate little table by Winnie's chair. Winnie patted his arm. "Tell Daddy Fay he ain't needed here," she quietly told him. "He can get to his own business now."

The boy left and Winnie served the tea. Helen took her cup and saucer as Winnie poured for the others. The room was decorated in pale-blue carpet and flowered wallpaper, a menagerie of taxidermied beasts, a bobcat, a beaver, a turkey with its breast puffed out. Then the women all stared at her, and Helen wasn't sure if they meant for her to talk.

At last, Winnie said, "Jorgen's a good boy."

Helen nodded. "Always liked him."

"But let me just say a few things. Things you may not understand," Winnie said. "'Cause our Jorgen's the best of all of us, my opinion. I know a mother shouldn't have favorites that way, but he's always been special." She sipped her tea, glanced off at the parlor's doorway. "Some different than them others. That's Jeremiah out on the porch. He's tame enough, but don't have much a mind. Different from my oldest. You knew Harlan?"

Helen nodded. Harlan was a known felon, served twice in the state prison for battery and drugs.

"Harlan was hell to raise." Winnie chewed her lip. "Past few days I been thinking about a coon dog Harlan once kept," she said. "Skittish blue, would tuck its tail whenever Harlan come around it. Well, Harlan didn't care for it so skittish, so he beat that dog. To toughen it up, you know. Lots of folks do dogs that way, I suppose. But them beatings just made it cower all the more, which made Harlan all the madder. The more he beat it, the more it shook. Till he took a wrench and broke its skull. Was but fifteen then, still a boy." Winnie set aside her teacup. "Never been more ashamed of one of my children, the way he done that dog."

She touched her own cheek, her eyes turned into the window's light. "You think some are just bad or evil or whatnot, but somewhere along the way they was someone's baby, suckling the teat like anybody. Then something puts a volt in 'em and they ain't the same no more. You might think a man like Harlan don't care much what his mama thinks. But I shunned him and he couldn't never shake it."

Winnie's eyes dropped and she crossed her legs, seemed to fold in on herself. Then she looked up, rolled back her shoulders. "You got children?" she asked Helen.

"Never got around to it."

Winnie nodded. "Didn't imagine so," she said. "You was never one took to affection, as I recall."

Helen eyed her, knowing she'd meant malice.

Winnie glanced at the young woman beside her. "Sheila," she said, and nodded at a big girl with green-streaked hair that spilled down her shoulders. "Sheila was Harlan's wife. Is his widow now. Widow come three days."

Helen watched the girl's blank expression, trying to understand what she was being told.

"Was Jorgen what killed her husband," Winnie said, her jaw set firm. "What killed his own brother." She motioned to the girl Helen saw at the cabin. "Beside Sheila sits Luanne. She's Jorgen's girl. Was meant to be married the fourteenth of October. Ain't that so?"

"Yes, ma'am," the girl squeaked.

"Never much cared for autumn weddings myself," Winnie said, sadly, staring hard at Helen. "You see them there beside each other? With what's between them, sitting there like sisters?"

Helen clutched her saucer and cup, watched them intently.

"This is Delmores," Winnie said. "We ain't the savages some say we is. Sometime things go crooked, but good or bad we get it straight. Nothing to concern the law, what with so much else to bother with."

The light outside was fading. Helen could no longer see Winnie's eyes. "You say Harlan's dead?"

Winnie's head cocked to one side. "Why you're here, ain't it?"

"No, it ain't."

Winnie inhaled deeply, uncrossed her legs.

"Jorgen missed a court date. Up in the city. Drug charge."

"Well," Winnie sighed, *"damn."* Her head swung to the side, her gaze settling over the younger girls. "We talk to them boys about not getting junked over. Fay's hard on that, says he catches them boys junked he'll put 'em under hisself. Harlan was weak on that, running days so junked you could smell it on him. Had to wash him three four times 'fore the smell come off him to be buried." She raised a long finger. "But not Jorgen. Drugs? No, that ain't right." She eyed Jorgen's girl. "You know about this?"

She fingered her nose ring, shrugged. "Weren't his."

"Harlan's?" Winnie asked.

The girl sniffled, said nothing.

Winnie clasped her hands together, her head bowed like she might pray. "Jorgen had this dog, you see. White pup no bigger than a squirrel. Carried that dog like it was made of eggs. Didn't want it wandering the woods or getting into nothing, so he kept it tied to the porch, right close to the house. Then Harlan come driving in here all junked over. Damn near hit the porch. Come on up to the house like weren't nothing happened. Asked if I'd make him fried chicken." Winnie shook a finger, then her hand became a fist. *"Fried chicken.* Thought of killing him myself. Ain't ashamed to say it, that dog beneath that truck, just as broken as a thing could be."

The tremor in Winnie's voice unnerved Helen. Gently, she set her cup on the floor and settled her weight on the balls of her feet.

Winnie slowly stood, the room dark but for a shim of twilight across the ceiling. "Ain't no law can touch what's been done here," she said. "You go on now, Helen. Go on and leave us be."

Helen's eye twitched and she tried to still her fear, patted the air with her hands. "Just here to talk, Winnie. That's all. Can't we sit back down, work this out."

Winnie put her face in her hands, heaved deep quaking breaths.

"I'm sorry, Helen. I'm just so sorry," she sobbed. "I've buried my firstborn, and now my most precious child is out there like an animal. Just found him ourselves yesterday. Out there running the woods, eating bugs, taking after livestock. I'm afraid he's broke." Her body shook as she began to cry. "He come home from that war and it weren't him no more. Oh," she moaned, "I miss him. Miss him when he's right there in the same room. Even when he's in my arms he ain't there." She pounded a fist against her thigh. "My precious baby and now he's broke. Broke and running wild and my heart's broke and there ain't no goddamn law to put that right."

Helen stepped to Winnie, grabbed her wrists. "I can help."

Winnie shook her head. "You can't."

"I can find him. I know where he'll be."

Winnie's eyes rose up searing. "Then what? Put him away like you done your mama?"

Helen flinched at the words.

"Help how?" Winnie's eyes bulged in the darkness. "Shoot at him? Lock him up like you done his cousin? His cousin what only come to look after a wounded soul just a little."

Fury overtook Winnie's face. She yanked her hands free and slapped Helen stiff across the cheek. Helen stumbled a step backward, touched her stinging jaw. Then she felt a collapsing, a weight in her chest, the gravity of her swollen heart. Her nostrils quivered. Her eyes melted. She couldn't let them see her cry. Helen pushed past Winnie, tears slicking her cheeks as she dashed down the lightless hall and banged out the screen door.

She leapt off the porch, landing hard and falling, then rising and racing through the beehives and into the dark chute through the woods and down the drive.

At the end of the drive, Helen stepped over the chain, rushed to her car. The windows were shattered, the tires slashed. The dashboard was a mess of wires, the radio gone. Struck sober, weeping, Helen pulled out her cell phone. She stared long at the glowing numbers, but couldn't figure who to call.

Winnie howled from back in the darkness, yelling Helen's name. Helen closed the phone, wiped her eyes. Her cheek burned to the touch. Winnie called again, closer now, and Helen briefly read the stars to get her bearings, then broke into the trees.

Helen ran through the woods, glancing back, again and again, into black briar and boles. The stars were blocked by trees and she navigated the hollows by memories made in daylight. She figured if she just kept going she'd find it, and then she did, the swath in the woods cut long ago, a gully cleared for power wires.

The wires bowed silent above her as she followed their path. Soon the wires flanked a field. Helen walked a fallow corrugate at the field's edge, the wires split off to wooden poles and then to a dark house atop a little rise. Helen kept her distance, crossed a rusted metal plank over the irrigation ditch, stayed with the wires through Gunnar Stovelund's low field of wheat. Behind Mavis Lott's place, llamas waggled their ears, their long necks bent as Helen rested against a tarred wooden pole.

Tower to tower she trod, down through flood-ravaged woods, fingers of moonlight fanning through leafless trees, clothes and feed sacks in the jigging branches, a shower curtain swaying like a spirit. Trees uprooted left sodden bunkers, roots thick as thighs corkscrewing out through the darkness. Debris everywhere, an orange traffic barrel, a picnic table overturned, plastic shopping bags rustling in the briar.

Helen waved away mosquitoes, climbed a slope with the urgency of knowing where she was, hooking her elbows around trunks, hauling herself up. Soon she stood on a ridge, out of breath against the leg of a power tower, a single cloud covering the moon, a blush of light from a window of the stone farmhouse on a far hilltop the only light that was not stars.

Helen emerged from the stand of hickory and into the pasture. Cows stood silent as she climbed through them, asleep on their feet as the history in their blood instructed. At the edge of the yard, Helen paused, steadying her heart, quieting her lungs, then scurried past a birdbath and a beneath a crabapple tree to stand against the house.

Like a thief, she slid behind a hedgerow and crouched under the window. Helen peeked over the sill. Candles lit the room. She could see old Moss Strussveld on the sofa, his arm dangled over the arm-rest, his fingers nearly touching the floor. He still wore his shirt buttoned at his throat, his straw hat tipped over his face. Helen could see his wife there beside him, a stout woman in a dark patterned dress, reading aloud from a book.

Though the window was open Helen could not hear the woman's voice. For a hushed minute, she watched. Then, with great care, Helen lowered herself to the dirt. Moonlight glazed the house's stones. Power wires stretched from the roof and out into the night. Helen's face ached, her sternum throbbed, her eyes straining to stay open as she settled in for the wait.

Helen stirred upon hearing a scuttle in the pasture. She'd sat for a long time. Pain tore through her tender chest as she turned onto a knee to stand. Through the window she saw the room in the house was now dark. She heard the cows lowing, bawling, and Helen stepped out from the hedgerow and crossed the yard to the edge of the hill.

The moon was well past meridian, bright and full, and down there, bathed in its light, ran a shadow, cows scattering, a figure throwing itself onto a cow's back. The cow cried, bucking. The figure was thrown, then rose again, chasing down another, planting his heels and twisting a calf's neck until it fell. Helen stood transfixed, cows rearing, grunting, the figure charging into their necks, shoving their heads, mounting one and riding it until it dropped, the man heaving, then staggering as if drunk to clutch the next about the neck, letting it drag him up the hill. Then the man's grip gave and he flopped to the ground and didn't rise. The cows lowed, trotting to gather in the darkness near the woods.

Helen looked behind her at the little stone house. The old man stood there in the window. She wasn't sure he could see her and didn't wave, merely turned and sidestepped down the hill.

For some time, she watched from just beyond the boy's reach, his face pressed into the hillside, his head below his boots, his body quaking ragged breaths. Helen said his name, but he didn't budge. She walked to his side, stood over him, his back slashed with scars, dotted with bruises, a gash along the base of his shaved head.

Helen sat on the ground beside him. The boy moaned, his breathing deep and lurching. She lay a hand between his shoulder blades. His skin burned and Helen let her palm take his heat.

Jorgen Delmore turned to Helen's touch. He lay his head in her lap, whimpering, his skin seeming to vibrate as she caressed his back, blood crackling through her own throbbing veins, and in a blink she drew up her eyes to see the lights, guttering in the distance far below, the electric lights of town shining in the darkness.

Delmore went without struggle, and together they plodded down the pasture hill. They followed the trail of power wires, skirted an algae-scummed pond, followed a stream that gurgled beneath an old stone bridge that shouldered the road. Once on the road to town, the parched breeze wafting the scent of fertilizer, Delmore asked, "Ain't you got a car?"

"It's broke," Helen said.

The road split fields planted so late with corn the stalks were no higher than a crotch. Seeing over the fields to the houses, lights bright here and there, the world seemed small.

"You missed your trial," Helen said.

"Oh."

"The marshal's to take you in. Be here at sunup."

The boy nodded. With his head shaved, he looked ancient. He smelled like turned earth. They walked side by side, down the crumbled asphalt and between the sleeping homes. A light was on in Henry Jamison's front parlor. Helen could see flowers out on the dinner table, a china cabinet against the wall. A light shone behind lace curtains in the Bressons' kitchen window, a light on in Treet Haskell's garage. They passed the Baptist church, its roof wrapped in tar paper, scaffolding surrounding the frame of its new steeple. The road sloped and banked, then flattened. The Old Fox Tavern lay dormant, its windows and doors boarded over. A raccoon trotted out of the gravel lot and crossed the road. Then Helen could see the lights from the brownstones.

They walked up the strip, the trash barrels brimming, cans and bottles lining one curb, the barbeques hunkered down at the far end. The diner's roof sign was burning red. The grocery's lights were on, too, light pouring onto the walkway through its glass door, slashes showing at the edges of the plywood filling the window. Helen had the keys to the store, asked Jorgen if he wanted anything.

"Could use a beer."

Helen entered the store and wove back to the beverage cooler. The freezers had switched on, the fans humming behind the glass. She grabbed a six-pack of Bud, saw the ice cream down the way. She looked a moment, took up a box that displayed a rainbow of popsicles. It'd been a while since she'd smoked, but she pocketed a pack of menthols from behind the register, put the rest in a paper sack, then shut off the lights and locked up the store.

Delmore sat on the curb, a little tabby cat nuzzling his fingers. She handed him a beer and he thanked her. They crossed to the side alley and took the stairs up into the sheriff's office, the door thrown wide, the lights left on. The jail door lay on the floor, broken off its hinges. Light from the cell softened the shadows of the main room. The place smelled like lavender.

Helen pulled her desk chair around to the window, pulled another chair for Delmore, and they sat looking out at the diner's red sign tinting the rooftop across the road. Helen got herself a popsicle, gave one to Delmore. It'd melted and refrozen and it took a while to pick the paper clean. She lit a cigarette and took a long draw, then licked the popsicle, and that seemed about perfect.

Delmore bit his popsicle, too, and in the room's light she could see just how filthy he was, smeared in muck, grass stains on his forearms, cuts across his sunburned forehead. Helen licked her popsicle again, was suddenly exhausted. She sobbed once, then felt as if she were shriveling, like a stabbed tire leaking air. She tried to breathe, gritted her teeth to stifle it all. Delmore stared out the window. Helen drew long on the cigarette, breathed, drew again, then snuffed the cigarette on her boot heel.

She slowly released the smoke, said, "Sorry."

He bit his blue popsicle, said nothing.

Helen wiped her eyes on her shoulder, watched Delmore suck on a chunk of ice. "You remember my mama?" she asked him.

He turned his eyes to her.

"She ain't well. Not at all."

"I liked her."

"I ain't well, neither," Helen said. "Maybe none of us are."

He nodded.

She looked out at the night, studied their reflections in the window's glass, two figures lost in the stars, the moon not the moon but a white globe of light hung above their heads. Jorgen held the beer in one hand, the popsicle in the other. He drank from the beer, rested the can on his knee.

"Back in the army," he said, "had this sergeant who was kind of a squeaky type. Had these little round glasses. Always trying to get me to read this or that. Nice fella. Everybody liked him, I guess. One day we had some shit go down. A sniper. Lost three of our own, just like that." He snapped his fingers. "Then we was all just sitting around, getting drunk. Sarge comes up in the bunch of us, says there's two worlds. One world was like it was back home, where folks ate cheeseburgers and kids had sleepovers and ball games and people went to work and got angry over stupid shit that didn't matter. Like their TV ain't no good, or they ain't got the right sneakers. Some shit like that." He held his popsicle stick to his lips. "But then there's another world, where folks ain't got a goddamn thing, and these motherfuckers'll try any damn thing to blow your ass to dust. Sarge says it was up to us to keep them worlds apart, and if we thought shit that happened over there wouldn't make it back to some little girl's sleepover then we had our heads full-way up our asses."

Jorgen bit the popsicle stick, then eyed the tooth marks in the wood. His face sagged. "Supposed to rally us, I guess." He shook his head, stared at the top of his beer. "But then I had to go back out that next day and the next and all I come to think on was how I ain't never had no sleepovers or ball games or none of that shit, and didn't none of it make a damn lick of sense."

Popsicle juice dripped down Helen's hand. She licked the heel of her palm, tossed the popsicle in the wastebasket. Then she rose and stepped to the window. She leaned her shoulder against the glass, glanced back at Delmore. His head hung low, his lips blue from the ice. He was just a boy, should be swimming in the quarry, smooching girls out in the Indian caves.

"My mama showed you how to mount a bird proper. That's something you had."

He rubbed his cheek. "Forgot about that."

"I still have that pheasant somewhere."

"Was a long time ago."

"No, it wasn't."

Delmore chewed the popsicle stick, rested his chin on his hand.

"Mama used to work three jobs," Helen said, maybe not even talking to Delmore. "Gave more time to others than her own. Raised myself mostly. When she was home, she'd be feeding the animals or baking something, hoeing the sweet corn. I thought she was crazy." Helen looked at her hands, callused and bruised. "Back when I was just a teen and full of piss I was mad at her about something or another. I remember her darning a pair of stockings and I says to her, 'Why don't you ever take a goddamn break? Enjoy life for a while?' Her eyes were sleepy and she barely looked at me, says, 'Can't go around with holes in your stockings.' So I says to her, 'What the hell's it matter? Keep your shoes on won't nobody know there's a hole in your stocking.'" Helen grunted a sad laugh. "She had this look you didn't want to get and I got it then, and she says, 'That the kind of woman you gonna be, Helen-Marie? The kind what walks around knowing they's holes in her stocking?'"

Delmore took the stick from his mouth, swigged his beer. He rubbed a hand over his sweating scalp, then stood and crossed to the window. He set his forearm against the glass, leaned his head against his arm. The night was waning, his eyes drawn to a welt of pastel light on the eastern hills.

"You got a shower I could use?" he asked quietly. "Clean myself up some 'fore that fella gets here?

Helen considered the boy in his stance, and the storm clouds in the near distance, their undersides lit pink. "All right then."

———

Helen kept the lights off in her apartment, ashamed of its unfinished walls, the milk crates holding her things, the mattress on the plywood floor. Delmore needed a shirt, so she gave him the baggy gray T-shirt she slept in. She gave him a pair of tube socks fresh from the pack. Gave him a towel and washcloth, a bar of soap, told him he could use the razor by the tub.

The bathroom window looked out over the fire escape, the grassy lot below strewn with lumber and broken bricks and colorful swatches of refuse she couldn't discern. Helen drew down the shade, used a wrench to turn on the water since the new fixture hadn't been installed.

Then she turned to him, the light dingy but his eyes a striking blue. "Let me know if you need anything."

Delmore stilled his eyes, nodded.

Then Helen went out and lay on her little mattress. Wrapped in a yellow bedsheet, she gazed out the window, listening to the water from the shower. Morning had risen dark, the sky a sheet of tufted iron. Light throbbed in the folds of clouds.

The shower ran for ten minutes, fifteen. The dust of the world rose and the rain was a smell before the first drop splattered against the window. The rain fell steady and the sounds from outside and the shower fell into a cadence. Then there was only water.

Three months back, the flood nearly covered this building, this room soaked brown and buckled. Helen imagined the water rising again, slowly filling the grocery, and then the office one floor down, the jail cot floating until waterlogged, then sinking, the water seeping between floors, through drywall and insulation, through plywood and nails.

Twenty minutes passed, the shower still going. Helen pictured the boy bounding through the high wet grass toward the woods, her nightshirt soaked, his scars washed clean. But she couldn't make herself get up to check the bathroom.

I just need a little rest, she told herself. Just a few minutes to gather myself. Then she imagined God in Heaven just as weary, slouched on his golden throne and deciding to try a smaller flood or two just to see if we'd save ourselves and spare him the effort.

Helen was by no means devout, but she knew the Bible, knew the story of God drowning the wicked world. As a breeze misted in through the window, she hugged herself in her thin sheet and pondered what she'll do if this rain keeps on and the people cry their end, the sun choked, the power towers submerged, and God's thunderous voice pierces the gray dome, charging a volt into that sacred truth behind her eyes. Will she think herself crazy? Cower and weep? Or will she rise from her damp mattress, hold stiff her trembling chin, and be the one?

The author would like to thank the following people for their assistance and support in making this book possible: Mary O'Connell, Wendell Mayo, Richard Messer, James Park Sloan, Eugene Wildman, Robert Olmstead, Mitch Wieland, Elise Blackwell, Alvin Greenberg, Janet Holmes, Bob Kustra, Anthony Doerr, Luis Alberto Urrea, Michael Collier, Benjamin Percy, Joy Williams, Michael Cluff, Tom Weekes, Danny Cerullo, Nick Steiner, Brandon Grew, Ryan Mann, Christina Thompson, David Lynn, Ted Genoways, Michael Ray, Otto Penzler, Scott Turow, and Nat Sobel. Thanks to the Bread Loaf Writers' Conference, the Tin House Writers' Conference, The Cabin, and the Idaho Commission on the Arts. Special thanks to Steve Woodward, Fiona McCrae, the Graywolf staff, and his agent, Sarah Burnes.

© R. Heathcock

Alan Heathcock's work has appeared in *Zoetrope: All-Story*, the *Virginia Quarterly Review*, the *Kenyon Review*, and *Best American Mystery Stories*, among other places. He is the winner of a National Magazine Award in fiction. A native of Chicago, he teaches fiction writing at Boise State University.

Book design by Rachel Holscher.
Composition by BookMobile Design and Publishing Services,
Minneapolis, Minnesota. Manufactured by Versa Press
on acid-free recycled paper.